REASON for CONCERN

ANITA KULINA

BRANDT
STREET
PRESS

Reason for Concern: A Mrs. B Mystery

by Anita Kulina

© 2019 Anita Kulina

Published by
Brandt Street Press
5885 Bartlett Street
Pittsburgh, PA 15217
www.brandtstreetpress.com

ISBN: 978-1-950836-01-7
Library of Congress Control Number: 2019944248

Book Design by
Mike Murray
Pearhouse Productions
Pittsburgh, PA
www.pearhouse.com

Cover Art by
Marci Evancho Mason

Printed in the United States of America

REASON for CONCERN

Sunday

1

Mrs. B sat on the front seat of the blue Mustang convertible, tying a yellow babushka under her chin. She looked in the side mirror to brush down her white bangs while her friend Anne tapped pale pink fingernails on the steering wheel.

Anne said, "What's taking Alice so doggone long?"

Mrs. B looked around. From where they sat, she could see most of the restaurant's parking lot. Almost all the cars from the Burchfield Senior Center Supper Club, which would have been more aptly named the Lunch Club, had cleared out already. A bigger-than-life tiger sculpture sat in the middle of the lot, flanked by a 12-foot lion tamer in top hat and tails, perennially pointing invitingly toward the entrance to Barnum's.

Mrs. B said, "I wonder why they have a tiger instead of a lion."

"What?" Anne was still tapping her fingers.

"You'd think they'd have a lion instead of a tiger."

Anne ignored her.

After a minute Mrs. B said, "Maybe tigers were cheaper."

Anne waved her arm in the direction of the parking lot. "Look. We're the last ones here now." The one remaining car from their little Senior Center convoy was pulling away.

"We ought to check the ladies room," Mrs. B said. "She could be indisposed."

"Oh, I didn't think of that. Let's go see." Anne shut off the engine and put the keys back in her pocket as she swung her long legs out into the parking lot.

It took Mrs. B a bit longer to get out of the car. The Mustang was in beautiful condition but it was an old car and it sat low, and the arthritis in her knee was acting up again. Oh, well, a walk around the restaurant might help. She removed the yellow scarf and tossed it into the car. She picked up her little yellow patent-leather purse, looked around, then shoved it underneath the seat.

Anne stood for a moment, admiring the old convertible. Then she said, "I don't know why I'm being so cranky. We can figure out how to get home. I don't have to follow them. And it's a beautiful day for a drive. We really couldn't have had a nicer day. Gosh, that heat wave we had."

"Wasn't that awful," Mrs. B said. Mrs. B had actually fainted from the heat a couple of Sundays ago. Thank goodness she was sitting on her glider when it happened. If Jimmy hadn't been hosing down his porch and come over to see what was the matter, she might have thought she'd just fallen asleep after feeling a little dizzy. Instead she woke, embarrassed, with her neighbor holding a cold, wet dishtowel to her forehead.

Today was a beautiful day, though. Anne was right. It was a perfect day to enjoy these winding country roads. The sun shone down brightly through the tall trees that bordered the parking lot, and there were just a few tiny clouds hinting at the edge of the horizon. The temperature hovered around seventy-eight degrees, blessedly cool for July.

Now that they were close to Barnum's front door, they could hear circus music from a speaker near the entrance. If Mrs. B was home right now, she thought, she'd be sitting on her porch eating a popsicle. She tried to remember if she had any popsicles left in her freezer.

It took a second for their eyes to adjust after the bright sun outside. Other than a couple of servers preparing for the dinner crowd, the dining room appeared to be empty. A young woman sat at a table near the entrance, folding napkins. When she stood, Anne waved her back down. "We already ate here. We're just looking for our friend."

The two women headed down the hallway to the far end of the restaurant. Straight ahead they could see sunshine through a propped-open door. They passed a glossy tan door adorned with a big, burly strong man and opened the bright pink one with the tutu-clad tightrope walker.

No one was inside.

A young man in a long white apron tossed a cigarette to the ground as he came through the back door. The ladies watched him enter the kitchen, then Mrs. B walked out the door he'd just come through. Anne followed.

A narrow asphalt strip ran the width of the restaurant. To their left was the parking lot, and to the right a row of pine trees. Almost directly in front of them was a narrow dirt path that went down a hill into the woods. At either side of the path's entrance were two large, prickly bushes. Mrs. B peered down the path but all she could see was trees.

Anne reached toward a bush. "Look, raspberries!" She ate a few, then picked some more.

Mrs. B filled her own palm and the two of them ate as they walked the perimeter of the restaurant, careful to be sure the berry juice didn't stain their summer outfits.

"I don't know Alice very well," Mrs. B said. "Is she the kind of person who would do this, disappear and you'd have to go look for her?" She pulled an old, faded blue handkerchief out of the pocket of her yellow blazer and wiped her hands.

"Beats me, I never talked to her before today," Anne said, then added, "Well, that's not entirely true. I used to see her down the Legion Hall but that was years and years ago, when I was married to my first husband. You know, on Saturday nights when they used to have the dances. We would say hello to each other there. But then her husband died, I remember he was only thirty-nine, can you believe it? Heart attack."

"That's so sad," Mrs. B said.

"Two little kids, too. Alice never came down the Legion after that. I wasn't even sure she was still in Burchfield until she showed up at the Senior Center last week. Never see her at the supermarket. She must go to the one in Rockwood. And we never see her at St. Mary's. I think she might be Protestant."

Mrs. B was puzzled. "Didn't you talk to her at crafts last week?"

"No, no, remember, I was doing that silk embroidery with the mahjong ladies," Anne said.

"Oh, that's right," Mrs. B said. "I forgot. Did you finish that little purse you were working on?"

"Friday afternoon I stitched the last feather on the fan. It really turned out cute, I'll have to show you," Anne said as she reached for the berry-stained handkerchief. "You know, when you told me you asked Lily if the mahjong ladies could show me how to sew like that, I was a little mad at you. I didn't want to sit at their table. All those Chinese ladies. I never knew any Chinese ladies before. But as soon as I got used to it, I really had a lot of fun."

"I'm sorry for putting you in a spot," Mrs. B said. "I didn't realize."

Anne wiped her hands and handed the handkerchief back. "Oh, you were just being nice. I know I kept telling you and telling you I wanted to learn that silk embroidery. Ever since my first husband brought me back a robe from overseas. Oh, it was lovely, Edwina. I wish you could have seen it. Royal blue silk, you know, that heavy silk, with a big parrot all up and down the back." She swept her arm to illustrate. "That one lady, the chunky one who always wears purple, I don't know how to say her name, she was so patient, showing me how to do the stitches. Thank goodness for Lily, though, translating. We'd have done the whole week in pantomime."

Mrs. B folded the handkerchief so the berry stains were inside and put it back in her pocket. "Even with Lily's accent, I always understand everything she says."

The sun glinted off the lion tamer's big red coat as they rounded the last corner. "Poor Alice," Mrs. B said. "Didn't you feel bad this morning when we were all in our cars getting ready to leave and her name wasn't on the list for carpool? I guess it happened because she was so new, but still. She had to feel awful, standing there all by herself. I'm glad we had room for her in your car."

Anne said, "Always room for one more, that's my motto. But where the heck is she now?" They were at the front of the restaurant again, next to the tiger. A path at the end of the parking lot led to a sidewalk. A few little buildings were clustered along it, a block or two away.

"She must have gone home with somebody else," Mrs. B said. "You don't think she would have walked down to those shops, do you?"

"Let's check before we head home." They got back into the car, and Anne put her key in the ignition. "I'd hate to leave her stranded here."

2

Downtown Hopewell appeared to consist of three establishments. The first looked like an old-fashioned corner store. White plastic tables and chairs sat outside, apparently to allow patrons to drink the "Ice Tea" offered prominently in their signage. A large, stately oak tree shaded the building. On a telephone pole near the doorway, a poster advertised the county fair. Up above the poster sat a metal Greyhound Bus sign. The other two buildings were a doctor's office and a bait shop.

Anne pulled up along the curb outside the store. Mrs. B pulled her purse out from under the seat. As they got out of their car, the roar of two enormous black motorcycles made them turn and look behind them.

Two young men in leather vests parked at the curb. The shorter one, sporting a big grin and a mass of blond curls, gave a long whistle as he walked toward them. "Nine-teen *sixty* eight! This your car?"

"My grandson's. He's in the service. Afghanistan." Anne smiled back. "I told him I'd keep it in my garage, but you have to take them out once in a while, don't you?"

"Sure. Blow the carbon out." He ran his hand along the fender as he circled it slowly. "Baby blue. *Bay-bee* blue. This is one fine car. Original upholstery?"

Anne tilted her head to consider. "I think so."

He nodded toward Mrs. B, then held out his hand. "Haven't seen you ladies out this way before. I'm Boom." They both shook his hand while a large, dark man hovered over them. "This here's Tiny." Tiny looked at Boom, then nodded toward the ladies.

Boom said, "You ever need that Mustang serviced, you come out our way. I promise not to sneak it out for a drive. Or two."

Anne and Mrs. B both laughed.

As the men disappeared into the store, Boom said in a loud whisper, "Matches her eyes, don't it, Tiny?

That baby blue." Then he gave Anne a wink as the door closed.

When the bikers were out of sight, Anne whispered to Mrs. B, "What's that say on the back of their vests?"

"M.C., it said. I'd guess it's an insignia for a motorcycle club," Mrs. B said. She was looking at the poster on the telephone pole. "The county fair's today."

"Oh, yeah. The fairground's just over that rise." Anne pointed. "Always had to take the kids to the county fair when they were little."

"Me, too. Wasn't that a long day," Mrs. B said.

"The kids used to love it," Anne said. "Not me, so much. All those stinky cows."

"They did have funnel cakes."

"Oooh, good point."

Anne peered over Mrs. B's shoulder at the brightly colored poster. "When I was little, I always wanted to run away to the circus, like Toby Tyler. Didn't you?"

Before Mrs. B had a chance to answer, Boom and Tiny came back outside, each lighting a cigarette. When they got to the bottom of the steps, a woman in a white t-shirt and jeans opened the door and said, "Hey, Boom."

He turned around.

"You going down over the hill?"

"We can," Boom said. "Why? What do you need?"

"Tell the professor I got those solar batteries in?"

"Sure," Boom said.

He and Tiny walked by the ladies on the way back to their bikes. Tiny was even bigger close up. Mrs. B felt like a mouse next to an elephant. As the men drove away, they both nodded toward Anne and Mrs. B. The ladies waved.

Anne said, "I can't remember the last time I was winked at. They were good-looking young fellows, too." She walked toward the door of the little store, then looked back at Mrs. B. "So what exactly is a motorcycle club, I wonder. Like the Kiwanis? Or do they hold races and things like that?"

"Sometimes it can be a criminals club," Mrs. B said.

"Well, I thought those young men were nice," Anne said.

Mrs. B had to agree. "They were very polite."

"They were charming." Anne wouldn't be dissuaded. "You know, people aren't always bad just because they're criminals." She opened the door and they were hit with a blast of cold air. "Remember how nice New Cannington used to be when the Mafia ran it? You never saw drug dealings or muggings or anything like that. My cousins who lived out there didn't even lock their doors."

3

There were two steps to the store's entrance but they weren't a problem. Mrs. B's knee was already beginning to feel better. Inside, the first thing that caught her eye was the display of popsicles in the freezer case. Through a doorway at the far end of the store, they could see a kitchen where a teapot whistled little billows of steam into the air conditioning. The woman they had seen before shut it off and walked toward them, a potholder in her hand. She passed the hardware display in the back of the store and set her potholder next to a row of cigarette racks along the wall.

The counter where she stood held an old-fashioned brass cash register and a large glass pitcher of iced tea, covered with an immaculately white dishtowel. They looked oddly out of place next to the large plastic Serve-Ur-Self Soda sign and the lottery machine.

"Professor, he don't have a phone," the woman said. "Can you imagine, this day and age? Some strange folks out this way. Most of them are nice, though." She lowered her voice to a loud whisper and leaned toward Anne. "The professor, I heard he eats tiger lilies."

Mrs. B headed to the popsicles while the woman straightened the beef jerky display on the counter, still chatting to Anne. "Nice day for the county fair. Last year it was so stinking hot nobody wanted to go anywhere near the livestock. Blue ribbon or no blue ribbon."

Anne said, "We were just talking about those smelly cows. You're right, today wouldn't be as bad as those really hot days."

Cherry, orange, root beer. Mrs. B tore herself away to join Anne at the counter. "We're looking for our friend. We were wondering if she might have stopped into your store. She was wearing a red jacket and white slacks." Mrs. B looked at Anne. "That's what she was wearing, wasn't it?"

"Yes, that's right. She had a red polka-dot scarf around her neck, too." Anne made a motion of tying the little scarf.

The woman at the counter shook her head. Then she said, "I saw a lady in a red t-shirt outside with a couple of kids, waiting for the shuttle for the fair. Could that have been her?"

Anne said, "No, probably not."

"Thank you, anyhow," Mrs. B said as she walked back to the freezer case. Cherry, she decided. When she got back to the counter with her popsicle, Anne headed toward the freezer case, too.

"Hope you find your friend," the woman said as she rang them up. Mrs. B grabbed some little white napkins from a metal holder on the counter. "Does she have Alzheimer's?"

Mrs. B and Anne looked at each other, then Anne said, "No, no, it's not that. We just crossed signals somewhere."

"Oh, that's good. That Alzheimer's is terrible. My aunt wanders all over creation and people have to call us and tell us where to pick her up. Poor thing," she said as she handed them their change.

Outside, Anne looked at the car, then at her popsicle, and sat down at one of the little white tables. Mrs. B did the same. Little bits of sunlight speckled them when the wind blew through the leaves of the oak tree.

"You don't think Alice has Alzheimer's, do you?" Anne asked.

Mrs. B took the popsicle out of her mouth. It was as good as she'd hoped it would be. "I only have our ride up here to go by, but I didn't see any evidence of it. Did you?"

"She seemed fine to me," Anne said. "Of course, she didn't say much."

"It's hard to hear in the back seat. And then with the top down, it's pretty loud while you're driving along. I don't think I said much, either."

"Who did Alice sit with at the restaurant? Did you see?"

Mrs. B said, "She was next to Old Mike on the one side. I don't know who was on the other side of her. I couldn't see all the way down that long table."

"I'm sure she went home with whoever she was sitting with," Anne said. "Don't you think?"

"That would make sense," Mrs. B said. "Though it does seem odd she didn't say anything to us."

The street was fairly quiet. Four teenagers rode by on bicycles. A large truck drove by with some sort of farm equipment in the back.

"Don't you like how they sell popsicles now? Remember how we used to have to break them in half?" Anne's mouth was turning red as she ate.

Mrs. B nodded. "This is less messy."

When they climbed back into the car, Anne switched on the radio and turned the knob to the left, eventually catching Tony Bennett in the middle of "Rags to Riches." Mrs. B peered into the mirror on the passenger side. Her lips were red, too. She tied the babushka under her chin and settled back to enjoy the scenery on the ride home.

4

By the time they reached Mrs. B's house, the clouds they'd seen on the horizon had drawn closer. There was a parking spot in front of Jimmy's house next door. Anne pulled in. The light from Jimmy's television was shining through his screen door. He came out on his porch, saw who it was and went back in again.

Mrs. B looked over to her own house while she pulled her house key out of the little purse. There was a pretty pink glow as the lamp she kept on a timer shone softly through her living room curtains. Just as she turned to say goodbye, Anne shut off the engine. "Ooh, wait, before you go. I have that catalog in my purse. The one with that dress. I don't know if I want blue or green. Take a look and tell me what you think."

Mrs. B stood on the sidewalk. Porches were empty, and it was unusually quiet for a summer evening. Smells like rain, that's probably why no one's out, Mrs. B thought as she looked around. At the top of the street nothing stirred except an occasional branch on a tree, swaying in the cool breeze that was picking up. Far at the bottom of the street she could see someone walking. Mrs. Papp and her little Pomeranian, Fuzzball. Mrs. B watched her pick Fuzzball up and carry him into the house.

Maybe there's a storm warning. Maybe that's why no one's out. She looked up at the sky. Was that lightning, back behind the houses at the top of the hill? Maybe not. Then again, maybe. She looked down now, at the pretty ivory upholstery in Anne's grandson's convertible. "Don't you want to put the top up?" she asked Anne.

Anne surveyed the slowly darkening sky, then shook her head. "Nah. I'll make it home." She popped open the trunk.

There were two purses in it.

"Oh, look, I still have Alice's purse!" Anne said as she held up a large straw bag. "I forgot, she put it in here when I put mine in. Remember, we all talked about how smart you were to bring a little purse to carry. I completely forgot it was in here." She put it on the front seat of the car. "I have to remember to take this to the Senior Center tomorrow."

Something's not right here, Mrs. B thought. She looked at Alice's purse, then at the key in her own hand. "Wait a minute. How did Alice get into her house?"

Anne was rifling in the bottom of her big white purse. "Oh, she probably had her keys in her jacket. That's where mine were. I threw them in my pocket. Since we paid for everything last week, I almost didn't bring my purse at all. But, I don't know, you feel naked without it." Anne dug a rolled-up catalog from the bottom of the satchel and handed it to Mrs. B.

The glossy booklet was folded open to a model in a red dress, carrying a matching sweater. Squares of different colors of fabric showed alongside. Mrs. B ran her finger over the smooth page while she tried to imagine the dress first in green and then in blue. They were both pretty but she did prefer the blue. She told Anne so.

Anne looked at the dress again. "I think I will get the blue one." She tilted her head jauntily and said, "It matches my eyes." Mrs. B was still laughing when she waved from her porch as the car rumbled to life and Anne pulled away from the curb.

The house was a little stuffy from being closed up all day, so Mrs. B opened the kitchen door and put the screen door on the latch. A breeze wafted in.

In her bedroom, she emptied the contents of the shiny yellow purse onto the top of her dresser, then put the purse in the bottom drawer of her chifforobe. She kicked off her dress shoes and lined them up in the row of shoes under her bed.

She poured a cup of coffee left over from the morning and set it to warm in the microwave. Far away she heard the sound of thunder. She looked out the kitchen window but she couldn't see much. It was getting dark. She hoped Anne got home before it rained.

Mrs. B looked at her powder blue pajamas, then decided on the white ones with the pink roses instead. They had a longer sleeve, and it might be cool tonight. She slid into her slippers and put her wristwatch on the dresser.

The little bell on the microwave dinged well before she was done. She got her coffee out, opened the refrigerator and poured milk into her cup, then sat down at the kitchen table to finish her cross-word puzzle. Before long, rain began to batter the windows. She stood and watched it for a while. Then she shut the kitchen door and said out loud, to no one in particular, "I'll feel a lot better when I see Alice tomorrow at the Senior Center."

Monday

5

Mrs. B and Mike were two of the first people at the Senior Center today. They were already at the church when Father Sean opened the basement door. The nuns who made the morning coffee must have left before Father got there, because the large room was oddly quiet. Father left the door propped open. It was still cool from last night's rain and, without the hum of the air conditioners, the faint sound of street noises came through the doorway. A bouncing basketball was followed by laughter as a group of boys headed toward the public school playground. A truck growled down the avenue, rumbling as it passed.

"Did Alice ride home with you? After Supper Club?" Mrs. B took the rubber band off a battered pinochle deck in the center of the card table. Old Mike stood across from her, a white mug in his hand. The white paper tag from a tea bag dangled lazily over the rim.

Mike surveyed the table for a few seconds, then walked around to her right and lowered his lean frame into the chair beside her. "I thought she rode with you and Anne."

Mrs. B reached for a little tablet and pencil in the middle of the table and put them next to her coffee. "She rode out with us, but she was gone by the time we left," she said.

"Alice sat by me at supper, and we talked a little bit. Nice lady," Mike said as he stirred his tea. The spoon tinkled against the cup. "She got up around dessert, you know how people do. I don't think I saw her after that." He thought for a minute, then shook his head. "No, I don't remember seeing her after she got up. I don't know who she rode home with. Why do you ask?"

It wasn't taking long for the room to fill. A few ladies headed in, chatting as they walked toward the crafts table at the back of the room. Men trickled in here and there. A group of mahjong ladies walked in, laughing and talking in Chinese. Anne and Rose were right behind them. They waved to Mrs. B, then headed toward the crafts table. Anne carried two purses, her own and Alice's big straw bag.

"I just wondered. Anne has Alice's purse," Mrs. B said to Mike, lifting her blue coffee mug and taking a sip. "We didn't notice until we got home."

Old Mike looked toward the back of the room where the ladies were gathering. Shelves along the wall were filled with brightly colored bits and pieces for their crafting sessions. He took another sip of his tea. "Well, she should be here soon."

"Who?" Vic asked, leaning over to set a green coffee mug across the table from Mrs. B. A circle on the mug held the letters C-Y-O.

Mike put his tea down in front of him, next to the spoon. He moved the string with the little paper tag to the other side of his mug. "Alice," he said.

Vic's chair scraped against the green tile floor as he pulled it out. "Alice who?"

"Alice the-only-Alice-who-comes-here," Don said, setting a yellow coffee mug in front of the last folding chair, across from Old Mike. They all looked up. Don was sporting a black and gold Pirates cap. For the last few months he'd worn the same hat every day, a beat-up blue cap that said AFL-CIO. The change almost made Don look dressed-up.

Vic said, "That Alice from up top of Eleanor Street? I know who she is. Walks that mutt, Maizie, down the ball field. Scraggly looking thing. Must be fifteen years old."

Mrs. B finished shuffling the cards. She set the deck in front of Don. He cut them and turned to Vic. "Dog died," he said.

"Maizie died?" Vic's face had a look Mrs. B had never seen before.

Don was taking a sip of his coffee. He nodded without looking up. "Couple weeks ago. The wife told me."

Vic looked down at his mug and gave it a stir. What was left of his hair fell into his eyes but he didn't brush it back, and he didn't look up until Mrs. B finished dealing. In all the years she'd known him, this was the first time Mrs. B had seen Vic express emotion. Other than disdain, of course. It rattled Mrs. B a little. Maybe there was more to Vic than met the eye.

Mike arranged his hand, then set the cards on the table, face down. He scratched his head through his white hair and picked up his tea with both hands. "Nice hat, Don."

"Pirates game. Son got it for me," Don said, still looking at his cards. He moved this one here, that one there, then tapped them on the table and fanned them out. "25."

Don looked at Vic, who didn't look up. He turned back to Old Mike. "Son got the wife one of them Pirate parrots. Don't know why a grown woman wants a stuffed animal. Damn thing's on our bedroom dresser. Stared at me all night."

They all waited while Vic looked back and forth at his cards. No one spoke. Old Mike took a big mouthful of tea just as Vic finally said, "26."

Mike swallowed and bid without looking at his hand. "27."

Mrs. B checked one more time. Good cards this morning. "30."

After the bidding, the rest of the game, as always, was silent.

6

The pinochle game went long, partially due to Vic thinking a little too long about each play and annoying the rest of them. By the time they were done, lunch was already being served. Mrs. B put the tablet and pencil back in the middle of the table, then stood behind her chair and looked around the room. She couldn't see Alice from this vantage point. There were a lot of people at the Senior Center today. More than usual, it seemed. Probably because it was Summer Salad day, she decided.

Mrs. B's knee always acted up a little more after a rain, and her pink tennis shoes treaded slowly over the faded green tile floor as she carried her tray to the lunch table. Snippets of conversation about the trip to Barnum's the day before followed along.

"Didn't you love the circus music at the doorway?"

"Wasn't it a pretty day for a drive? I'm never out in the country anymore. We used to go out there every summer, to my Aunt Irene's farm. Well, she wasn't really my aunt..."

"I'm going to make a circus cake for the baby's birthday on Saturday. Our first great-grandchild, you know we have to spoil him."

Everyone seemed to be in a good mood, but even amidst the lively chatter, Mrs. B wondered again about Alice. And now she began to worry about the worrying. It wasn't like her. Mrs. B's son Leo had been missing for many, many years. She had no idea where he was, no idea what kind of trouble he might be in. Over time, through trial and error and the forfeit of sleep over too many nights, she had learned to carefully spend her days focused on the task at hand, giving Leo's fate to God through her nighttime prayers. She didn't know why Alice's absence was affecting her like this. For goodness sake, she barely knew the woman. And she was probably here, getting ready to eat her Summer Salad, even though Mrs. B hadn't yet seen her. She could just be in the kitchen, or in the ladies room.

When she reached her lunch table, Mrs. B set the beige plastic tray down between Anne and Rose, who had both already started to eat. Myrtle's merry voice was soothing, and Mrs. B allowed herself to get caught up in the cheerful conversation. How colorful their table looked! Four plates of green Summer Salad topped with chicken and little orange sections, four large glasses of iced tea. Four bowls of lime gelatin with maraschino cherries mixed in. What a pretty lunch, she thought, as she pulled out the empty chair across from Myrtle.

Little tufts of hair stuck up here and there around Myrtle's lilac hairband, and they wiggled as she talked. "Timmy's birthday was so nice, Ed! I was just telling Rose and Anne about it. I made coconut cake, that's what Ronnie likes, and Mary Beth got cupcakes from the bakery for all the little kids. They were so funny on that Slip 'N Slide! Billy and Timmy were really good the whole time, they didn't fight or anything. And Ronnie and Mary Beth are getting along so much better now. I love it when the family is all together." She took the last bite of her gelatin and got started on her salad.

Rose looked up at Mrs. B. "It looks like everyone had a good time at Supper Club."

"We met a couple of young fellows," Anne said. "One of them flirted with me!" She caught Mrs. B's eye and they both started to laugh.

Mrs. B said, "It really was a lovely afternoon. You know, Anne drove us in her grandson's convertible. I hadn't been in a convertible since before I was married. You might want to think about coming next time, Rose. I think you'd enjoy it."

Anne nodded encouragingly. "Supper Club really is a lot of fun." Rose's dark eyes smiled, and she looked as if she might actually consider it.

Anne said, "The restaurant was really something. It almost felt like you were at the circus. Everything on the menu had a circus name. The diet dish page had a picture of the thin man, and the spicy food page had a picture of a man being shot out of a cannon. The largest size of everything on the menu was called the elephant. The biggest hamburger was an elephant burger, the biggest French fries was elephant fries. They even had a cotton candy sundae in the desserts. Not a lot of clowns, though." She turned to Mrs. B. "I thought there'd be more clowns."

Mrs. B said, "Some people are afraid of clowns. I expect that's why."

"You're probably right," Anne said, nodding. "Anyway, it was very colorful. They have circus music playing by the door where you come in, and you can tell they gave a lot of thought to the way they decorated. The ceiling was red, white and blue stripes from the middle, like a circus tent, and everywhere you looked there was something to see. They had a unicycle in one corner with a stuffed monkey in a captain's uniform. In the back corner was a big stuffed giraffe. I can't say I ever saw a giraffe at a circus, but I suppose they have them sometimes. It really was darling, the whole place."

"I don't think you can go to the circus anymore," Myrtle said. "They said on 60 Minutes they put all the lions in a retirement home."

"It's just different now, I think," Mrs. B said. "Acrobats, tightrope walkers, that kind of entertainment."

"Ooh! Then maybe Father Sean can get someone to donate tickets so we can go to the circus," Myrtle said. "Next time they come to town I'll ask him."

Mrs. B ate one of her maraschino cherries and, since the table was quiet, decided it was okay to speak up. "Was Alice at crafts today?"

Anne said, "No, I didn't see her. Do any of you know where she lives?" She looked at Myrtle, then at Rose. Myrtle was stirring her iced tea with her knife. "We need to return her purse."

Rose said, "Why do you have her purse?"

Anne said, "She left it in my trunk. She drove up with us to Supper Club."

Myrtle put the knife down before she answered. "Alice, she lives up on Eleanor Street. Her Mary Jane and my Annie used to know each other. I don't know the address of the house but it has yellow awnings. There always used to be pretty flowers in the front yard. I don't have any flowers in my front yard. Just in the window box. I have purple pansies in the window box."

"Purple pansies are so pretty," Anne said. Then she turned to Mrs. B. "Eleanor isn't a long street. I bet we can find it. Do you want to ride up with me?"

Mrs. B did.

7

Clusters of peach lilies adorned the front of a little house with yellow awnings. Eleanor Street was paved with dull red bricks that buckled in places. The narrow road only had parking on one side, and Anne had to drive partway down the block before they found a parking space.

Anne grabbed Alice's big straw handbag by its tan leather handle. "Wonder why she brought this big purse?" She opened it and glanced inside. "There's hardly anything in here."

"It was probably the best one to match her outfit," Mrs. B said.

"Oh, I bet you're right," Anne said.

It was a nice block. Quiet. Little brick houses, one or two frame houses with aluminum siding. All of them small. Little rectangular front yards, all nicely kept. A glider on one porch. Two folding chairs on another, a little folding table between. In one yard a little black poodle played with a blue ball, then ran toward a grey-haired man. He tossed the ball again, calling to the dog in a foreign language that sounded familiar. Slovak, maybe. Russian? At the far end of the street sat a big house with a turret.

The ladies climbed two wide steps to the worn brick porch under the metal awning. "Nice and cool," Mrs. B said as soon as they stepped into its shade. To their left, two old, comfortable-looking wooden armchairs sat on either side of a little wooden table. Each chair had a faded plastic cushion, one pink, one yellow. There were pale rings on the table, probably left by dewy glasses of lemonade over many years of summer afternoons.

A white aluminum screen door opened to a wooden front door. A wreath of faded blue flowers in the shape of a heart hung above an old-fashioned knocker. Anne knocked. The knocker rattled, and the mail slot at the bottom of the door rattled with it.

There was no answer. She knocked again.

Anne bent down and peeked in the mail slot. "Looks like she picked up her mail."

"If it came yet," Mrs. B said, looking through the front window. "Maybe she's in the kitchen."

The little concrete pathway that led from the street to the porch took them around the house and up a little slope to a side door. Marigolds lined the path. The backyard was tiny, even smaller than the front yard. There was a little rock fountain along the back fence, surrounded by a thick border of tiger lilies and Queen Anne's lace. A table full of potted plants sat alongside the house.

"Pretty garden," Mrs. B said.

"It is. Must be a lot of work," Anne said.

"I think a lot of these are perennials," Mrs. B said.

The kitchen door was flush with the little sidewalk that led there. Anne held her hand above her eyes to shield them from the sun while she peered through the kitchen window.

Mrs. B could tell from where she stood that no one was in the kitchen. Through the tied-back blue gingham curtains was a gleaming white counter with a row of yellow canisters. At the end of the counter was a filled-to-overflowing spice rack, extra spices stacked neatly alongside. A doorway at the far end of the room led to what looked like a hallway. A long wooden bench was in view. A pair of green shiny boots stood beside it, next to a little bucket of gardening tools.

Anne knocked on the window of the kitchen door and they waited a while. She knocked again. They waited. Mrs. B looked around at the yard. It certainly was well cared for.

"Alice must have gone out," Anne said. She turned back down the path, carrying the straw purse by its long leather handle. Even as tall as Anne was, the purse almost touched the ground.

They walked back to the car. The grey-haired man was sitting on his stoop, still tossing the ball across the little front yard. The little black poodle wiggled its way back, waving the ball from side to side as it ran.

Mrs. B sat down on the hot seat. She said, "You have the convertible again."

"I like this car. It makes me feel good," Anne said as she tossed the handbag onto the back seat. "I'll bring Alice's purse down to the Senior Center tomorrow. It's too big to shove through the mail slot, and I don't want to leave it on her porch."

"That's a good idea," Mrs. B said, but truthfully, she didn't see anything good about this at all. Where was Alice? Where had she been since yesterday afternoon?

8

At home, since it was Monday, Mrs. B went to her dresser drawer and brought her bills and checkbook to the kitchen table. She wrote out a check for the electric bill and one for the water bill. She read letters from two different Catholic charities, then wrote a ten-dollar check to one and threw both letters in the recycling. She checked her math twice, put her checkbook back in the dresser drawer and counted out three stamps. The envelopes went in the living room, on top of her television.

She took a quick walk around the house. Everything looked fine. No housework she couldn't put off until another day. She looked in the hamper. The laundry could wait, too. It really made more sense, didn't it, to sit on the porch and read the book she was halfway through.

She poured a cup of coffee from the pot she'd made that morning. While she heated it in the micro-wave, she got the book from her bedside table. When she heard the little ding-ding-ding, she carried the book and coffee to her front porch and set them on the wide railing while she situated herself in the white wooden rocking chair near her front door. The rocker sat in her daughter's old room in the winter-time, but in the summer it was just the right thing for sitting outside.

It was a nice afternoon. Not too hot here on the porch, in the shade. The street was fairly quiet. Mr. Bacigal was tending his flowers. Betty Daley climbed her steps with a plastic shopping bag, then fussed a while on her porch before she opened her front door. Mrs. Papp sat down on the front stoop with her grandbaby. She waved. Mrs. B waved back.

Just as she'd opened her book to the page she had marked, two little girls came down from a porch across the street, looked both ways and then made a beeline toward her. The first child's flip-flops flapped as she bounced up the front steps. "Hi, Mrs. B!"

Mrs. B couldn't help but grin, as always, at her little neighbor's boundless energy. "Hello, Kelly. How are you today?"

"I'm good. This is Blossom."

Mrs. B nodded in the second girl's direction. "Hello, Blossom. Well, isn't that an unusual name. Is that your given name?"

Blossom knit her brow and looked at Kelly. Kelly shrugged.

Mrs. B tried again. "Is that the name you were christened with? Or is it a nickname?"

"It's my real name. My whole name is Blossom Marie Donegal."

"I'm pleased to meet you, Blossom Marie," Mrs. B said.

"Blossom's going into third grade, just like me," Kelly said.

Mrs. B hoped she hadn't made Kelly's friend feel uncomfortable. She wanted the child to feel welcome. A compliment was easy to find, and she gave it a try. "You have lovely hair, Blossom."

"She doesn't like it," said Kelly.

"You will when you're older," Mrs. B said. Blossom brushed a long red curl back from her forehead and tucked it behind her ear.

The two girls sat down on the top step of the porch, and Kelly leaned back on the railing. She said, "Blossom's got a dog."

"That's nice," Mrs. B said, opening her book.

Kelly said, "He's big and white."

"He's from Russia," Blossom said. "My uncle didn't want him anymore. He's good though. My dad had to train him. Now he only barks when someone's on the porch, and he doesn't jump up on anybody."

"That's good," Mrs. B said, half reading, half listening.

"His name's Spider," Kelly said.

Mrs. B looked up.

"He eats spiders," Blossom said.

Mrs. B went back to her book with the girls' chatter as lively music in the background, and the three of them sat on her porch until it was nearly suppertime.

9

By ten o'clock the air conditioner in her bedroom had been running for over an hour, and the room had cooled down. Mrs. B shut it off, climbed into bed and propped a pillow against the headboard. On the table next to the bed was a letter from her daughter that had come in the morning mail.

Helen lived in London. She was married to a nice man, Malcolm, who worked with her at the BBC. Mrs. B was very proud of her daughter. Helen was smart. Diligent. Ambitious in a carefully modulated way. And even though she wrote often, it was always a treat to read Helen's letters.

Mrs. B had been an only child. Her few remaining cousins had moved to Toledo years ago, and she had no one left on Polish Hill now. With Albert gone, and Leo away for so, so long now, her daughter was really and truly the only family she had.

Mrs. B so looked forward to learning what was new at Helen's office, what parties she'd attended, what new piece of furniture she thought she might buy. They didn't have a lot in common, Helen and Mrs. B. It had been fifteen years since Mrs. B had a new piece of furniture, and that was only because Mrs. Davern was moving and didn't want that tall table in her living room, and Mrs. B said she'd take it and use it as a telephone table in her hallway. Mrs. B wasn't interested in fancy parties, and even when she was a career gal she had no use for office politics. But she did love those letters. They made her feel connected to her daughter, sharing these everyday details of her life. When a letter arrived, Mrs. B would often set it next to her bed so she could spend the whole day looking forward to reading it.

This letter started off with a new restaurant that Helen and Malcolm went to, where they really liked the prawn dish but weren't so keen on the desserts. Then a description of the new curtains Helen was thinking of buying for her kitchen, and why she thought she'd like them so much better than the ones she had now, since the color had faded, and besides the blue in the new curtains matched the blue in her breakfast dishes even better than the blue in the old curtains did.

But then, somehow—Mrs. B couldn't put her finger on it—the tone of the letter changed. Helen began to talk about how much she liked the neighborhood where she and Malcolm lived, and how she wished her mother could live near them, but she knew her mother would never move to the U.K. Wouldn't it be nice, though, for Mrs. B to be somewhere pretty, with houses that weren't run-down and people who dressed nice, and no worries about whether the roof would leak the next time it rained? Someplace where there wasn't so much crime?

And then there it was. *Mom, have you ever thought about moving to one of those retirement villages outside the city?*

Honest to goodness, that Helen! She threw the letter down on her pink chenille bedspread.

Mrs. B had lived in this very house ever since she and Albert plunked a hard-earned $400 down on it the year they were married. They'd sent checks every month to the previous owner who'd moved all the way to Texas, and she was very proud that they had never missed a payment, even when Albert was laid off from his job at the mill. This house was their home. It was where they raised their children, including Miss Fancy-Pants Helen with her highfalutin ways.

Sure there were a few empty houses on their street now. Sure there might be a fight at the bar on a Saturday. Maybe now and then there was a burglary, but that was mostly drug addicts, and everyone knew who those poor boys and girls were. None of that made Mrs. B want to leave her home, her neighborhood. She'd lived here most of her life. She knew everyone in nearly every house on her street. St. Mary's Church was only a block and a half away, and there was a bus stop there, too. She had lunch with her friends every day at St. Mary's Senior Center. So what if her roof needed tending now and then? That was part of being a homeowner. This house was paid for lock, stock and barrel, and she was proud to call it hers. Why on earth would she want to move?

She picked up the letter again. When she read a little farther, Helen's motives became clear. Jimmy next door had written to Helen after Mrs. B fainted on the front porch during that hot spell.

Mrs. B's heart softened. Helen, God bless her, always wanted to fix things, even when they weren't broken. Mrs. B didn't know where that tendency came from. No one would ever accuse Mrs. B of coddling her children. She always gave them plenty of space to grow, even when it meant enduring the discomfort of letting them learn through their own mistakes.

Mrs. B first noticed this tendency in her daughter when Helen was still young. Mrs. B and her husband had an inconsequential argument, one Mrs. B probably wouldn't even remember if Helen hadn't gotten involved. It started when Mrs. B told Albert he shouldn't have bought that t-bone steak today because it wasn't even on sale and a round steak would have been just fine, and Albert said she was cheap, and Mrs. B said she wasn't cheap, she was frugal and there was a difference. That was it, and then Mrs. B went back to peeling potatoes and Albert went into the living room and sat in his easy chair to read the paper. Helen took it upon herself to run back and forth between the living room and the kitchen. *Don't be mad at Mama! Don't be mad at Papa!* They both had to assure the little girl that it was just a disagreement, no one was mad at anyone, sometimes people just disagree.

Helen was the same way with Leo. One Saturday when Leo was misbehaving, Mrs. B told him not to do it again and promptly forgot all about it. Afterward, she found Helen earnestly lecturing her little brother that his new paint set was to be used on paper on the coffee table, not to put spots on the living room wall.

In high school, Helen was always the student to tutor the boy who was failing algebra. She was the friend to find a date for the girl who wasn't asked to the dance. Helen-to-the-Rescue, Albert used to call her.

Things hadn't changed, apparently. *Have you gone to see a doctor,* Helen wanted to know. *You don't need to be outside on a hot day. That's why Malcolm and I bought you the air conditioner. You can open the door to your bedroom and let the air conditioner cool the kitchen. Then you can sit at the kitchen table and do your cross-word puzzle and you'll be cool and comfortable. You can look out the window. And you certainly shouldn't walk down to the Senior Center when it's hot out. You need to remember you're not young anymore, Mom.*

Mrs. B stuffed the letter back in the envelope. She reached over to her nightstand for a new romance novel and stuck the envelope in the back of the book. Helen did mean well, she reminded herself. She was irritating, but she did it out of love.

Tuesday

10

The next morning, between pinochle hands, Mrs. B craned her neck to see the crafts corner at the far end of the room. Anne and Rose were there, and she could see the back of Myrtle's head. Though she couldn't see the faces of all the ladies at the long table, she didn't see anyone who looked like Alice.

Mrs. B tried to concentrate on her cards. She had too much on her mind, and she was bidding high. Don was her partner and they usually played well together, but today she couldn't read his signals during the bid. It was her fault, she knew. She was trying her best, but it was so hard to focus. It made for a rough morning. Mrs. B never minded getting bad cards—it was bound to happen sometimes—but she hated when she lost because she didn't play well. Lunch couldn't come soon enough.

"I'm almost done with the decorations for my tote bag," Myrtle said when they sat down to eat. There was a big jar of sweet relish at the corner of her tray. It was covered with dew so she must have brought it straight from the Senior Center refrigerator. She put it in the center of the table, then wiped her hand on her pink shorts. "I just need to finish the big red flower for the middle. They'll all be so pretty when they're done, don't you think?"

Rose said, "Anne's will be the prettiest."

"Oh, Anne's will be so nice!" Myrtle turned to Mrs. B. "Ed, Anne's got a navy tote bag and she's putting white daisies on it." She turned back to Rose. "I like yours, too. That pink and purple look so pretty with the yellow. It's so cheerful."

Rose looked pleased.

Myrtle said to Mrs. B, "Thursday morning the teacher's coming back, she's going to show us how to glue the flowers on the tote bag. Then they have to sit for a couple days and then we can take them home. So next week we can take them home. I think I might keep mine in my living room. I can put all my ladies magazines in it. That way they won't be all over the place. They're all over the place now. If I put them in my tote bag, the living room will look all nice and redd up." She spread her hands, palms down, to illustrate, then reached for the relish.

Rose said, "It was nice of the dollar store to donate those bags for us to decorate. I bet it was Father Sean got them to do that. He's a sweet boy."

"I bet Father Sean paid for them himself," Anne said, biting into a carrot stick.

Rose looked surprised. "Do you really think so?"

Anne nodded. "I don't think he'd tell us if he did. And you know that guy who owns the dollar store. He watches everyone like a hawk while you're in there. And then he talks to you all nice when you get to the counter to pay."

"I didn't think about that," Rose said.

"I like Father Sean more than ever now," Myrtle said. "I just love that Irish accent. I can't understand everything he says but all his sermons sound so adorable. I want to pinch his cheeks sometimes, but you can't do that to a priest. Why did they give us carrots and celery sticks today? We usually get beans with a hot dog."

"I expect they were out of beans," Mrs. B said. She opened her little carton of milk, then turned to Anne. "Alice wasn't at crafts, was she?"

"No. I asked about her, and nobody's seen her since Supper Club. Carmella was sitting next to her, and she said Alice got up to use the ladies room and never came back. She figured she must have gone to sit by someone else."

"People did shift around a lot after we ate," Mrs. B said. "Don was next to us, remember, and he took his lemon meringue pie down to the far end of the table."

"People always do that at Supper Club," Myrtle said. "You want to talk to all your friends."

"So no one's seen Alice at all?" Mrs. B said.

"None of the ladies at crafts had seen her. Did you ask the card ladies?"

Mrs. B's pinochle foursome was the one serious card game at the Senior Center. Playing 500 Rum, especially with ladies who chattered throughout the simple game, held no fascination for her. She much preferred the challenge of pinochle, even if she did have to play with the men.

"I didn't think to ask them," Mrs. B said. "But I probably would have seen her. I did ask Old Mike if he knew who she went home with. He said he didn't see Alice after dessert came."

"Everybody moves around at dessert," Myrtle said. The mound of relish on her hot dog had spilled onto her plate. She dipped a carrot stick in it.

"I still have Alice's purse," Anne said.

"I thought you gave it back yesterday," Myrtle said, sopping the remains of the relish with a celery stick.

"Alice wasn't home," Mrs. B said. "I think we had the right house."

"Eleanor Street is so small," Myrtle said. "I bet it's the only house with yellow awnings. You don't see awnings anymore, not like you used to. Why is that, do you think? They keep the house so cool. We don't need them on my side of the street because we get the morning sun. The other side of the street, they could use awnings. Our porch is nice and cool."

"Let's go back up after lunch," Anne said to Mrs. B. "If Alice was shopping or something yesterday, she'll probably be home today."

Mrs. B took a bite of her hot dog and nodded. Anne was right. Alice was probably home. She was probably fine. Today when they knocked on the door, she'd probably be there. Mrs. B took another bite. She would feel so much better if Alice answered the door this time.

11

As they walked toward the church parking lot, Anne said to Mrs. B, "I didn't want to say anything in front of the other ladies, but I'm a little worried about Alice. You don't think anything's happened to her?"

Mrs. B was relieved to know she wasn't the only one. "I've wondered that too, but let's not get carried away. She's probably home, and we're probably going to see her in five minutes."

"I started asking about Alice at crafts today," Anne said as they reached the edge of the lot. The worn blacktop was cracking in places, and Mrs. B was careful where she stepped as she walked toward the silver sedan. Anne pressed the little gadget that opened the car doors, and it beeped as the buttons went up.

"You didn't bring the convertible," Mrs. B said.

"Yeah, my daughter saw me in it yesterday and gave me all sorts of what-for. 'That's supposed to be in your garage. What kind of a grandmother are you?' " Anne tilted her head back and forth in imitation as she talked. "Bobby wouldn't care, but you can't tell that to my daughter."

It was roasting hot in the car. Anne opened the windows. "So let me tell you what I heard at crafts," she said. "I brought Alice's name up, just asked if anyone rode home with her. Nobody had. But then Alice became the topic of conversation. How her husband died so young and she had to raise her girls by herself. We already knew that. But I learned some things about her daughters."

Mrs. B put no stock in gossip, and Anne knew that. Anne wasn't a gossip either. It was one of the reasons they got along so well. Mrs. B put on her seat belt. The buckle was hot. She shook her fingers when it was fastened.

"What about her daughters?" Mrs. B said.

"Jane and Tree. That's their names." Anne pulled out of the lot and turned down the avenue.

"Tree?"

"Short for Theresa," Anne said. "Jane is Mary Jane. She goes by Jane now that she's grown. They don't get along, apparently. The girls. Haven't since they were teenagers. Carmella used to live by Alice when the girls were in school. She said Jane wasn't even in Tree's wedding."

"That's sad," Mrs. B said as they started toward Eleanor Street. A cobblestone hill made the car bounce as they climbed.

There was a parking spot in front of Alice's house today. Next door, a woman in purple and white gardening gloves was pulling weeds from the border of a little front yard. She looked up for only a second, then went back to her work.

Mrs. B followed Anne to the front door. They knocked, but there was no answer. They walked around to the side of the house and peered in the window. Everything looked the same as it had the day before. The two of them went back to the sidewalk and turned to stare at the house.

The woman next door had a bunch of weeds in her hand. A straw visor sat low on her forehead. She pushed it up with the back of a glove and said, "You looking for Alice?"

Mrs. B nodded. "We're friends of hers from the Senior Center. Do you know where she is?"

"I thought she was home," the woman said, adding the weeds to a little pile on her sidewalk. "She's a homebody, Alice is." The woman took her visor off and wiped her forehead, then squinted up at the sun. "Sunny day like this, though, you'd think she'd be working in her garden. Or sitting on her porch reading. She reads a lot."

Mrs. B asked, "Could she be visiting her daughters? Do they live in Burchfield?"

"Oh, they live here, but she won't be there," the woman said, shaking her head while chopping at a dandelion plant with the point of a red-handled trowel. "Ungrateful little bitches."

Anne's eyebrows went up. Mrs. B said, "Could you tell us where her daughters live?"

"She won't be there, I'm telling you that for a fact." The woman wiped her gloves on her grass-stained shorts and waved an arm toward the opposite side of the street. "Tree lives over on Heath. White house with a shiny green front door. Looks stupid, if you ask me. I don't know why she wanted that green door. Looks like it belongs on a bank. Mary Jane lives back of her. The street that looks like an alley. Their backyards touch." The woman laughed and said, "I bet they hate that," as she picked up the pile of weeds and carried them toward a trashcan at the side of her house.

"Where's Heath? Over by the ballfield?" Anne asked as they got in the car.

12

The green door was oddly shiny. When they knocked, it sounded like it was made of metal.

No one answered.

Mrs. B stepped back to the sidewalk, past an overgrown hedgerow, to peer between the houses. She hesitated, then took a step forward down the long row of cracked cement that lined the alleyway.

The front of Tree's house was covered with white vinyl siding, but on the side it was faded brown insulbrick. Couldn't afford to fix up the whole house, Mrs. B imagined. She looked up. Two stories. Phone lines and cable wires strung their way from the second floor to the street.

She hesitated again, then walked a little farther, past two blue garbage cans, past a ladder lying on its side, past a big plastic bin. They must keep their tools in there, she thought. She smelled dirt now, newly dug dirt. A flaccid garden hose was attached to the side of the house, stretching back to a corner of the yard where a small pine tree sat in what was obviously its new home. Mrs. B turned toward the house. There was a tiny back porch, not much more than a landing. A dead potted plant sat alone on the railing. The kitchen door was shut and no lights seemed to be on.

From here Mrs. B could see beyond the backyard, to the yards of the houses on the next block. They were all surrounded by fences.

"It doesn't look like anyone's home," Anne said from behind her.

Mrs. B jumped a mile. "Anne! You scared the living heck out of me."

"You would make a terrible prowler," Anne said.

Mrs. B pointed through Tree's chain link fence. "That white house back there, with the blue trim? That might be Jane's. That one or the red one next door. Both of them border this backyard." She turned around. "Come on, let's get off of these people's property. We're trespassing."

It was a short block and it didn't take long to go around it. They pulled up alongside the white house just as a woman in a pink blouse opened the front door of the red brick house next door. The woman seemed to be in a hurry. She pulled her brown hair back into a stubby ponytail while she walked toward an old truck in a grass-bordered cement driveway.

Mrs. B walked around to the driver's side. The truck was a dull yellow except for the front right fender, which was a dull red. There was a smell. Oil, maybe. "Excuse me, is this..." Mrs. B pointed toward the two houses but looked at Anne when she realized she didn't know Alice or Jane's last name.

Anne took over. "We're looking for Alice Childers. Do you know where her daughter Jane lives?"

The woman climbed into the truck, then turned toward them, all smiles and dimples. In a sweet voice she said, "I'm Jane."

"Oh, good," Mrs. B said, relieved. "We're friends of your mother. From the Senior Center. We haven't seen her for a couple of days. Do you know, has she gone away?"

"Goodness, dear, I don't have any idea," Jane said as she put the windows down. "She just lives a few blocks over, on Eleanor Street. 254. The house with the yellow awnings."

"We were just there," Mrs. B said. "She wasn't home. Do you know how we might get in touch with her?"

"Sorry, dear, really wish I could help you. I have to pick my boyfriend up at work, otherwise I'd love to stay and talk. Wish I could. You ladies have a good day now, hear?" She started the engine. It rumbled loudly.

Anne rolled her eyes at Mrs. B as Mrs. B knocked on the truck's door. Jane looked toward them, tilted her head. The dimples popped out again.

"Does your mother have a cell phone?" Mrs. B asked.

"I don't think so," Jane said. "Got to go. Sorry I couldn't be more help. You have a nice day today!" She began to back out of the driveway, and Anne and Mrs. B both stepped quickly away. The truck gave a sharp bounce as it hit the road, then it turned and took off.

Anne shook her head. "You'd think you'd know if your own mother had a cell phone."

Mrs. B watched the truck's red brake lights come on as it reached the stop sign at the corner. "You would," she said, "wouldn't you?"

13

Driving back, they passed Tree's house again, just as she was opening her green front door, two blue plastic grocery bags on the doorstep beside her. A blonde girl, maybe a year or two older than Kelly, walked ahead of her and into the house. A watermelon was wrapped tightly in the girl's arms.

"Look," Anne said as she pulled in at the curb. She waved at Tree, and the two ladies got out of the car and climbed three green concrete steps to the porch.

Tree was taller than her sister, and darker. The short hair and black t-shirt she wore made her seem tougher, but there was definitely a family resemblance. Tree probably had dimples too, if she ever smiled. She wasn't smiling now.

Mrs. B looked at Tree's porch furniture, but they weren't invited to sit. The three of them stood in a half-circle on the cool cement porch. Its floor had been painted in green enamel, though not the same shade as the bright green door. Darker. Mrs. B thought, I bet this is slippery when it rains.

"I haven't laid eyes on my mother in weeks," Tree said when they asked her. "I don't know where she is."

"We're a little worried," Mrs. B said.

"Well, I've got my own problems," Tree said. "My old man went out of town Sunday on a job and didn't even tell me he was going. Can you believe that? Left me a note on the kitchen table. Like I'm his goddamn cleaning lady."

The words came out of Tree with such fury that Anne and Mrs. B both took a half step away from her as she spoke.

"So when's he coming back?" Tree said. "He doesn't tell me that. Is he answering his phone? No. Not when *I* call him, he isn't. So who's going to cut this grass? These hedges are all over the walk. Look at them! How's the mailman going to get up to the house? Huh? And who's going to have to cut them? Me. Me, me, me. I have to do everything around here. Goddamn him."

After an appropriate pause, Mrs. B said, quietly, "Your sister Jane hasn't seen your mother either. We thought you might be worried."

Tree said, "I got my own problems."

The three of them stood on the porch in awkward silence. Finally Tree looked down at the groceries and said, "I gotta get supper on."

The ladies crossed the street toward their car and, when Mrs. B looked up, Tree was still on the porch, watching them. They locked eyes for a second and then Tree shouted, "Why do you care where my mother is? Like it's any of your goddamn business!" and slammed the door.

"Lovely girl," Anne said.

"What do you think happened to Alice?" Mrs. B said.

"That's the million-dollar question," Anne said.

"We need to find her. I feel responsible," Mrs. B said.

"Me, too," Anne said.

14

It was raining after supper. Mrs. B had the kitchen door open as she sat at the table with a cup of cooling coffee. She was almost done with the crossword puzzle when Kelly and Blossom walked in from the hallway.

"Your front door was open but you weren't in the living room," Kelly said.

Mrs. B looked up, still deciding whether she had the right answer to 4 down. "I was in here," she said.

"We came to visit you," Kelly said, sitting down at the kitchen table.

"Yes, I noticed that," Mrs. B said. She went to a hutch in the corner to get three little plates. "Kelly, move that newspaper so Blossom has somewhere to sit."

Blossom sat down and Kelly stacked the newspaper on a far corner of the table. Mrs. B put a plate in front of each of them. As she reached into the cupboard for a box of store-bought cookies, she said, "Kelly, get the milk out of the fridge."

Kelly opened the refrigerator door and put a quart of milk on the table. "Do you want me to get glasses?"

"Please," Mrs. B said as she put two cookies on everybody's plate.

"Two or three?" Kelly asked, two short, squat glasses already in her hands.

"Two. I still have coffee," Mrs. B said, sitting down again.

Kelly carefully poured two glasses of milk and gave one to Blossom, who immediately drank a big gulp. Kelly went to sit down, but Mrs. B looked at her and she put the milk back in the refrigerator first.

"Guess what. Blossom's sleeping at my house tonight. Spider, too," Kelly said.

Mrs. B erased the answer to 4 down. "That's nice," she said.

"Spider's watching TV with my mom."

"That's nice," she said again.

Kelly ate half of a cookie with one bite. When she was done chewing, she said, "We walked down here all the way from Blossom's house. Just me and Blossom. And Spider."

"Is that far?" said Mrs. B. She took a sip of her coffee and then got up to put it in the microwave.

"It's six blocks. We counted it," Blossom said.

"Well, that's a nice little walk," Mrs. B said. "Are you allowed to do that all by yourselves?"

"We have to bring Spider," Blossom said.

"We saw you on Blossom's street," Kelly said. "You and another lady. You were talking to Cassie's mom. I was gonna yell hi but Blossom said don't." She looked over at Blossom but her friend was swallowing another big mouthful of milk. "'Cause Cassie's mom's mean," Kelly added.

"She's scary," Blossom said. She had a little bit of milk on her lip and wiped it off with the side of her hand.

Mrs. B looked over at the girls. "Scary?"

"Yep," Blossom said. "Last summer my mom got me a badminton set at the dollar store. I only had it one day and the birdie hit their front window and Cassie's mom came out and yelled at us and took it in the house. I didn't tell my mom. She'd yell at my mom, too. She yells at everybody. Cassie gave it back to me later. Cassie's in fourth grade. She's not mean like her mom. She's nice like her dad. I never play badminton anymore, though. I don't want Cassie's mom to yell at me. She says bad words and everything."

Mrs. B nodded her head in sympathy. She'd found Tree a little scary, too. "It's best to stay away from people like that," she said.

"These are my very favorite cookies ever, Mrs. B," Kelly said, reaching for another.

Mrs. B grinned. "I seem to remember that," she said.

15

Mrs. B went to bed at ten o'clock but at eleven she was still wide awake. It was cool enough to sleep, but sleep wouldn't come.

No sense just lying here, she thought. She turned on the light and blinked a few times. It seemed much brighter than it did during the day. She slid into her bedroom slippers and shuffled to her dresser for the stationery box. She looked through the drawer for her favorite pen but couldn't find it, so she went to the kitchen and got a ballpoint from the junk drawer.

She would write a nice long letter to her daughter. Tell her all about Supper Club. A lighthearted letter might be just the thing. She wouldn't say anything about Helen's letter yesterday. She'd just pretend she didn't get the letter, unless Helen asked. That was probably the best way.

Mrs. B sat at the kitchen table. She could hear an occasional car outside, but otherwise the street was still. Through the window over the kitchen sink she could see Jimmy's back porch. A rake sat near his kitchen door. A dim glow shone through his dining room window.

What if it had been me instead of Alice? What if I had disappeared when it was time to go home? She knew the answer. Anne and her other friends would look for her, and they wouldn't stop until they found her. But of course they knew Mrs. B, and knew her well. They would know she wasn't the type to wander away, or to leave without saying anything.

Anne and I shouldn't have left Hopewell without Alice. We shouldn't have assumed she went home with someone else, even though it seemed logical at the time. We should never have left until we found her. That's something you learn in kindergarten. Stay with the person the teacher paired you with. Stay together. Never let your partner out of your sight.

This is our fault.

Of course, Alice is probably fine, isn't she? I'm probably making a mountain out of a molehill. Most likely she's at home sleeping right now. We probably just keep missing her when we stop by.

She looked up at the clock near the doorway, then beyond it to the Last Supper on the kitchen wall, above the table. She and Albert bought it years ago at the Catholic bookstore downtown. She thought back to the night when they ate their very first dinner in their new home. Steak and fried potatoes, with baked apples for dessert. Halfway through the meal, they both looked up and realized they needed a picture of the Last Supper for the wall. The room wouldn't be complete without it.

There had been an assortment of Last Suppers to choose from—standard framed copies of the Da Vinci painting, modern interpretations, reliefs in plaster and metal. The one they finally chose was a copy of the Da Vinci that adorned a rustic slice of wood. It really was beautiful, they both thought so. She remembered Albert hanging it proudly on the kitchen wall and when he did, it made her feel all warm inside. It made the new house feel like it was really, truly home.

Mrs. B folded back the vinyl tablecloth, her summer one with the pink flowers, revealing its fuzzy white backing and the old wooden table underneath. She opened the box of stationery. Her favorite pen was inside.

This thing about Alice, if nothing else, was peculiar. Why wasn't she home the last two days when they knocked on her door? Why didn't anyone at the Senior Center see her after dessert on Sunday? Where would the woman go without her purse? And sadly, and maybe most importantly, why were she and Anne the only ones who seemed to care?

Mrs. B took a look at her coffee pot, then went to the refrigerator and poured a glass of milk instead.

Well, she couldn't do anything to help find Alice while she was sitting at her kitchen table at eleven o'clock at night. She could write this letter to Helen, though. She knew her daughter meant well. She didn't want Helen to worry about her. A chatty letter might be just the thing to ease her mind.

She set a little stack of pretty paper in front of her and took hold of the pen. Everything in this letter should be lighthearted, Mrs. B decided. She'd tell Helen all about the decorations at Barnum's, and how they drove there in Anne's grandson's convertible. She'd tell her what a pretty day it was, and how they sat outside afterward and ate popsicles.

What else? Something innocuous. She could talk about the weather. No, better not. It might make Helen think about that hot spell and get all worried again. Better stick to the circus decorations and the convertible.

I'll tell her about Kelly's little friend Blossom, Mrs. B thought as she began to write. I'll tell her about Blossom's pretty red hair.

Wednesday

16

Alice wasn't at the Senior Center the next day, either. Mrs. B and Myrtle were on kitchen duty, and Mrs. B waited until they had almost finished cleaning up before she finally asked her friend, "Myrtle, do you know Alice well?"

"My Annie knew her Mary Jane," Myrtle said, wiping the kitchen counter in neat little circles with a red and white checkered dishcloth. "She was over the house a couple times. They were teenagers, though, so her mom didn't bring her over. She came with Annie. It was when that whole thing happened with her sister. I remember she was crying and I thought, 'Well, you can't cry over this. You're the one who didn't want to go steady.' That wasn't right, I thought."

Mrs. B was wiping the outside of the dishwasher. She wrinkled her nose and stood to look at her friend. "I don't understand, Myrtle. Who didn't want to go steady?"

"Mary Jane." Myrtle turned on the water in the sink.

Mrs. B put her hand on her friend's arm. "Wait a minute, Myrtle. Stop for a second and tell me this again."

Myrtle shut off the water and turned toward her, the dishcloth still in her hand. It dripped onto the floor and she wrung it out in the sink, then ran the water again. "You know," Myrtle said. "When Theresa Childers married that boy from the Cream King."

Mrs. B said, "Myrtle, stop a minute. Just for a minute."

Myrtle shut off the water, put the dishcloth in the sink and wiped her hands on her apron. She turned toward her friend and tilted her head as if to ask, What?

Mrs. B said, "I'm sorry, Myrtle. I have no idea what you're talking about."

Myrtle stared at Mrs. B, then started again, slowly and deliberately. "Alice," she said. "You wanted to know if I knew her."

"Yes," Mrs. B said.

"And I said I didn't know her but I knew Mary Jane. She was at the house with my Annie when that whole thing happened with her sister."

"What thing?"

"You know. The thing with her sister." Myrtle said the last three words slowly and deliberately, then picked up the dishcloth again.

Mrs. B took it from her gently and laid it on the counter. "I don't," she said.

"You have to know," Myrtle said. "Everybody knew about it when it happened. You probably just forgot. Remember that boy that used to work at the Cream King, Greg something? The one that looked like Archie from the comic book. He was Mary Jane's boyfriend and then she kissed this other boy up in the bleachers during a football game or something. I think it was a football game. Maybe it wasn't a football game. Anyhow, he started dating Theresa. Greg did, the Cream King boy." Myrtle picked up the dishcloth again, wrung it out and wiped the front of the refrigerator.

Mrs. B followed her. "Oh," she said.

"And then Greg and her got married, and then they didn't talk anymore. Her and Mary Jane," Myrtle said.

"Who got married?"

"Theresa. What did they call her? Tree. She went by Tree," Myrtle said. "I knew it was a funny nickname. We always used to say Terry for Theresa. I wonder why she didn't go by Terry? Terry's a pretty name."

"That's why Alice's daughters don't speak?"

Myrtle nodded. "Mary Jane wasn't even in Theresa's wedding. You should always have your sister in your wedding," she said.

Growing up on Polish Hill, Mrs. B was surrounded by extended family, including lots of cousins around her age. She remembered her Aunt Minnie had a strict rule that if one of her daughters went out with a boy, no other daughter was allowed to date him. Aunt Minnie always told them that boys would come and go but sisters were forever.

"That's a sad story. Your sisters and brothers should be your best friends," Mrs. B said.

Myrtle was washing out the sink. She rinsed the cloth and folded it, then hung it over the faucet. "I'm glad my kids all get along," she said.

17

There could be lots of reasons Alice wasn't at the Senior Center today, Mrs. B thought as she turned the corner and walked toward home. Alice might have simply decided to do something else the last couple of days. Lots of people skipped coming to the Senior Center from time to time.

Alice only joined the Senior Center a week or so ago. Maybe she decided she didn't like it. Maybe she felt unwelcome when they accidentally left her off of the carpool list.

Mrs. B always walked up this side of the street, past the pussy willow trees. A few doors up from the corner, a rustling sound made her turn her head.

"Afternoon, Ed." Hap Morgan was on his porch reading the newspaper, his pipe upside down in an ashtray next to his chair.

"Afternoon, Hap."

"Hot," he said, turning to the sports section.

Mrs. B nodded. The summer sun peeked from behind a bank of puffy clouds, then went back into hiding. It wasn't much more than 80 degrees out but it felt hotter. Muggy.

It was possible Alice was home when Mrs. B and Anne stopped by. Maybe she didn't hear them knock. She could have been cleaning her upstairs, or taking a nap. She could have been down in her cellar doing laundry.

It didn't smell like laundry, though. Usually if someone is doing laundry you can smell it.

Mrs. B stepped higher as she passed the spot in the pavement where a tree root made the sidewalk buckle. Across the street, the front yard of an abandoned house was filled with wild daisies and Queen Anne's lace.

Her knee hurt a little bit. Mrs. B considered it for a moment. Not enough for an aspirin, she decided. More an ache than a pain.

Dr. Washburn said she was supposed to walk every day. Maybe the distance to the Senior Center and back wasn't far enough. Tomorrow she'd walk an extra block or two up the avenue before she came home. Then when she had her check-up with the doctor on Friday she could be honest and say she'd started walking for exercise, and she intended to keep it up.

It was possible, she supposed, that Anne or Mrs. B had inadvertently done something to offend Alice. That could be the reason Alice didn't answer her door when they knocked. Mrs. B thought about that for a minute. She couldn't think of anything they could have said, but the truth was, you couldn't always tell. Some people were very sensitive.

Alice didn't seem the sensitive type, though, from what she could judge through the little bit of conversation they'd had. She seemed likeable. Friendly.

Across the street, Mr. Bacigal had planted snapdragons again in the little green patch between his sidewalk and the street. Pink buds danced in a welcome breeze, and some sort of red flower climbed the trellis from his tiny yard to his front porch.

His poppies last month were so pretty. Mrs. B always loved when his poppies were in bloom.

The tinkle of childish laughter caught her ear as she climbed the five steps to her front porch. Kelly and Blossom were in front of Kelly's house, a big white dog lying patiently at their feet. That must be Spider, she thought. He did seem well-behaved. The dog's leash was stuck under a rock that Mrs. B was sure he could pull away from without even trying. He was on the landing underneath them, head on his paws, tail in the air.

The girls looked up and waved. Mrs. B waved back.

She'd give Anne a call in an hour or so, Mrs. B decided. They should check at Alice's house one more time. They should call directory assistance, too, and see if Alice will answer her phone. She didn't know why she didn't think of that before.

It was a few degrees cooler in the shade of her front porch. Mrs. B picked up the newspaper and took it into her kitchen, but it was hotter in there. She opened her back door to let some fresh air through the screen, put the screen door on the latch, then went back to the front porch. She set a little glass of orange juice on the railing next to her white wooden rocker, then sat down to read the newspaper.

Before she got past the front page, she'd made a decision. If Alice wasn't home again today, it was time to get the police involved. Someone had to locate the poor woman, and it didn't look like it was going to be her daughters.

18

It was still hot out at seven that evening when Anne and Mrs. B walked into the #4 Police Station, carrying Alice's purse.

The building was smaller than Mrs. B remembered. Its nondescript entrance of yellow stone made it look kind of like a garage. The door was propped open, and when the women went inside they immediately knew why. No air conditioning.

It was dark inside the entrance. Shadowy. The worn counter was fairly high and had a little swinging door to the right. Three desks were on the other side. Two faced each other, and at each was an officer.

One, a young man, was working on the computer. The other officer had a fistful of papers in her left hand and was rifling through a drawer with her right. The third desk was empty. At the far end of the station was a glassed-in office, which looked no less dreary than the rest of the place. For the captain, Mrs. B supposed.

The officer with the papers pulled a stapler out of the desk drawer, then stood up when she caught sight of the ladies at the counter. The woman was middle-aged and her hair was jet black. Her blue uniform fit a little too tightly, but the blouse and slacks were neatly pressed. She wore her hair pulled back in a big clip behind her head.

"Can I help you ladies?"

Anne put Alice's purse on the counter as Mrs. B said, "Our friend is missing."

"Pardon me?" The policewoman was looking at the big straw handbag.

Mrs. B said, "Our friend has been missing since Sunday afternoon. We've been trying to return her purse. We checked her house but no one's home. Her next-door neighbor hasn't seen her and neither have her daughters. No one has seen her since Sunday."

The officer nodded, then dumped the contents of the purse onto the counter. There wasn't much in it.

A wallet with fifteen dollars. A tube of lip balm, a package of tissues. A half-eaten roll of breath mints, the paper folded over neatly at the used end of the roll. A tan change purse filled with coins, mostly pennies.

"So her daughter isn't here, why?"

Mrs. B and Anne looked at each other. Mrs. B said, "We were worried. We thought we would come and check."

"But you've talked to the daughter?"

"Yes, both of the daughters. She has two," Anne said.

The officer went to her desk and came back with a spiral pad. "Give me her daughter's name and phone number."

Mrs. B and Anne looked at each other, then back at the officer. Anne said, "We went to their houses. We don't know their phone numbers."

The officer held a ballpoint pen over the pad. "Give me a name, then."

Mrs. B didn't know Tree's last name, and Jane might be the better bet anyhow. "Jane Childers," she said. "I think her last name is Childers. On Iverson Way."

The policewoman began to type on the computer. Anne tapped Alice's purse as she watched her, then picked up Alice's wallet.

"Oh, look, this must be Jane and Tree." Two high-school photos were side-by-side in their little plastic windows. "Look at those hairdos."

"No picture of her granddaughter," Mrs. B said.

"That's sad, isn't it. You'd think her daughter would have at least given her a school picture," Anne said.

Something blinked and Mrs. B looked up. The fluorescent lights, hanging from rods in the ceiling, blinked again, then settled down to their orange glow. She looked at the photos of Alice's daughters again. "They're both pretty girls. They look even more alike in these pictures. They could almost be twins, except for the hair color."

"Tree's taller, don't forget," Anne said. "They're both wearing too much eye makeup."

Mrs. B pictured the little crowd of teenagers who used to spend their summer evenings in the ice cream stand's parking lot. "The girls you'd see at the Cream King usually did wear more makeup than they needed."

Anne rifled through the rest of the items in the wallet. "Alice's Medicare card isn't in here. Don't you keep yours in your purse?"

"I always have it with me. You need it for the bus." Mrs. B was a little uncomfortable looking at Alice's things without her permission.

Anne was examining Alice's voter's card. "Maybe she doesn't take the bus a lot. Maybe she only puts it in her wallet when she's going to the doctor." She picked up the breath mints. "Know what my favorite breath mint is? Sen-Sen. You can hardly find it any more. I asked Tony to carry it at his store but he said nobody buys it." She looked at the breath mints again, then set them back on the counter. "I'm going to check the next time I go to Sarris Candies. I bet they have Sen-Sen."

The officer hit a button on her phone and both women turned as a dial tone hummed through the speaker. She punched each number with the eraser of a long yellow pencil, and the phone was answered on the first ring.

"This is Officer Ramsey, #4 Police Station. I have two ladies here who want to report your mother missing."

"Those nebby old women!" Jane's voice was almost unrecognizably shrill as the policewoman grabbed the receiver. The officer across from her looked up from the computer, then back at his work.

"Uh-huh," the policewoman said, glancing quickly toward the counter and away again. "Uh-huh. Uh-huh." Pause. "Yes, ma'am, that's true." Pause. "Yes, ma'am." Pause. "Okay, ma'am." Pause. "Yes, ma'am. We'll do that." She hung up the phone and looked at it for a while before she approached the counter where they stood waiting.

"Ladies, I wouldn't worry about your friend. Her daughter said she took a vacation. She probably just forgot to tell you." She put the items back in Alice's purse and handed it to Anne.

As they turned to leave, the policewoman spoke again. The businesslike tone was gone now, and her voice was soft and kind. "There isn't a keychain in here, did you notice that? Your friend probably went home after she saw you on Sunday, changed purses and left for vacation. I'll bet she's sitting on a beach right now, having a wonderful time."

Thursday

19

Myrtle took one bite of her banana pudding and said, "Eww."

Mrs. B looked at hers skeptically. Anne and Rose both dipped their spoons in.

"Oh, my goodness, that's awful," Rose said. Anne wrinkled her nose and put her spoon down again.

Just as Mrs. B said, "I'll take your word for it," Carmella walked over to their table. She leaned between Rose and Anne to address all of them and whispered, almost conspiratorially, "I'm walking up to the Cream King for dessert. Anybody want to join me?"

They all said yes. Even Rose.

They couldn't leave just that minute. Myrtle, Anne and Rose had to store their tote bag projects on the shelves along the back wall, and then they had to say goodbye to the ladies at the crafts table. Carmella joined them, and Mrs. B thought about it, but she knew they'd be a while once they started talking. She went to the kitchen and grabbed a dish-towel. It wasn't her turn for clean-up duty again until next week, but she might as well make herself useful while she waited. She was glad she did. It was a full half-hour before they got out the door. By then the kitchen was spic-and-span and Mrs. B felt she'd earned her ice cream.

The little cadre of ladies walked up the short slope to the avenue, then turned the corner past the Grill. The door of the bar was propped open and its sweet-sour smell wafted toward them. The group of men who were perennially on the sidewalk outside the Grill parted politely when they saw the ladies approaching, and hellos were exchanged. Mrs. B glanced inside. The bartender and another man were watching one of those judge shows. She looked at the sidewalk, mildly surprised. There were more men outside the bar than there were inside. It was a pretty day, though, so maybe that was why.

They could only walk one at a time past the bar, what with the men on the corner, but as soon as they got to the bank, there was more room on the sidewalk. Anne and Rose walked ahead with Myrtle weaving between them, chattering away. Carmella and Mrs. B took their time and fell into step together at the end of the little parade.

Carmella lived in Rockport now, but she'd lived in Burchfield most of her married life, and she'd been coming to St. Mary's Senior Center for quite a while. Mrs. B didn't know Carmella well, but they always said hello. They saw each other at Supper Club, and they sat together a couple of summers ago when the Senior Center went to a baseball game. Mrs. B sat next to Carmella a few months ago, too, when she made one of her rare expeditions to the crafts corner. The teacher showed everyone how to make beaded bookmarks that day. They turned out not to be very practical, though they were pretty. She sent hers to Helen, and now it was hanging on the bulletin board in her daughter's office at the BBC.

They passed Tony's store. Mrs. B spotted Patrick, Tony's son, through the window. She waved, and he waved back. Carmella said, "Alice Childers didn't quit the Senior Center, did she? I haven't seen her all week, and I was so happy when she joined."

So Mrs. B and Anne weren't the only ones who missed her. "I don't know," Mrs. B said truthfully.

Carmella said, "Alice was always such a homebody, it surprised me when she came down to the Senior Center last week. I guess with Maizie gone. Even with her garden and her books, she probably needs more to keep her busy. I bet she's lonely without that little doggie. I hope she comes back to the Senior Center."

"Me, too," Mrs. B said. More than you realize.

"I used to live up by her," Carmella said. "Before my mother-in-law passed and we moved down to her house in Rockport. Then I hardly ever saw Alice anymore, except once in a while when I ran into her at the Shop and Save. We go to the one in Keyport. It's a little farther but they have good sales. Last week they had city chicken, buy one get one free. You hardly ever find city chicken anymore."

Mrs. B didn't want to talk about city chicken. She said, "Do you know who Alice rode home with after Supper Club? She rode up with Anne and me, but she didn't ride home with us."

"No," Carmella said. "I never talked to her after dessert. You know how everybody moves around.

Anyhow, I hope she comes back to the Senior Center. She's a very sweet lady. Smart, too."

They passed Dr. Washburn's office. The door was shut. The building had glass block windows, so they couldn't really see anything inside. The lights were on.

Mrs. B hesitated for a second. Oh, for goodness sake, she decided, just ask. "Carmella, what did you and Alice talk about at Supper Club?"

Carmella didn't seem to think it was a strange question. "I don't know, regular stuff. All the circus decorations. How much we liked going to the circus when we were little kids. Romances." She pointed across the street at a front porch. "Those are pretty glider cushions, aren't they? I wonder where they got those."

They were in front of Lefty's insurance office now. Pirates, Steelers and Penguins paraphernalia were plastered all around the border of the big front window. Lefty was talking on the phone at his big green metal desk, holding the receiver with his right hand, gesturing wildly with the other. He looked up and waved as they walked by. They both waved back.

Mrs. B turned to look at Carmella. "Romances?"

"We used to swap them when I lived by her," Carmella said. "We had shopping bags full. We were talking about the new ones we got. We like the same kind, me and her. The real romantic ones. We don't like those ones where everybody's having sex all the time. It's so much nicer if they leave that to your imagination, don't you think?"

"I feel the same way about movies," Mrs. B said.

They passed the empty lot, then the building where the bakery used to be. Carmella said, "The bakery in Rockport's closed now, too. You can hardly find a real bakery anymore. Don't you wish we still had bakeries everywhere? Of course we'd probably all weigh 20 tons if we did." Carmella started to laugh. "We'd be waddling up the avenue." She puffed her cheeks and stuck out her elbows, swaying from side to side. Mrs. B giggled. Anne and Rose turned around to see what they were laughing at, but then Myrtle called them and they walked ahead to see what she was looking at over by the beauty parlor.

Carmella said, "A lot of women would have turned bitter, having your husband die and having to raise the kids all by yourself but, you know, I never heard Alice complain. Not once. She did what she needed to do around the house, all on her own. Amazed me how she could fix stuff. Her husband wasn't dead a year before she put a light in, up over the dryer in her cellar. Got a book that told her how. The woman put her own garbage disposal in, can you believe that? Nowadays she'd have probably gone to school to be an engineer or something but, you know, you didn't do that in our day. Everybody told you no one would want to marry you if you were too smart."

"That's true," Mrs. B said.

"I can't even change the batteries in the television remote," Carmella said. "If my Frank dies, I'll have to sell the house and move to the senior high rise." She stopped and leaned against the wall of the building where the dry cleaner used to be, then took off her sandal and shook it. A little stone fell out. "I sure hope Alice comes back to the Senior Center. She's one of those people, always looking at the sunny side. You feel good after you talk to her."

Mrs. B said, "You make me sorry we didn't get to talk much in the car on the way to Supper Club. She sounds like the kind of person I'd like to get to know better. Anne took us up in her grandson's convertible, and we had the top down."

"You can't hear anything in a convertible with the top down," Carmella said. "Oh, you'll love Alice when you get to know her. It's so nice to be around someone with a sunny disposition. You know, at

Supper Club some of the ladies at our end of the table were saying they thought it was disgraceful to date at our age, and Alice spoke up to say she didn't agree. 'Everyone should believe in love,' that's what she said.

"See, that's what I mean about her. And her being alone all these years. It's so sad her little Maizie died. All Alice had was that dog, her daughters being the way they are. Maizie loved her and she loved Maizie."

"Sad, about her daughters," Mrs. B said.

"The way those girls treat her," Carmella said, "it's awful. I have to say, though, I saw it coming. Alice did for them too much. Tried to bend over backwards after their dad died. They would sass her right in front of people, Jane and Tree both, and Alice would never say a word. Later, she'd even apologize for them. 'It's hard for my girls with their daddy gone.' Well, it was hard for Alice, too, but those girls never showed her any mercy. Treated her like dirt. And then that whole thing with the boyfriend, and Tree ends up marrying him, and their grandma holding everything together. Then Mrs. Oliver died and the whole family went to pot."

"Their grandma?" This was the first Mrs. B had heard about a grandmother.

They were in front of the new beauty parlor now. It had smoky gray windows and gold lettering on the door. The tinted windows made it hard to see more than big round bulbs of light near the ceiling and some sort of activity inside. Music played faintly. Jazz, it sounded like. The whole effect was elegant and completely out of place with the rest of the avenue, like it had been dropped there unintentionally.

Carmella said, "My granddaughter cuts my hair."

"I go to that place by the supermarket," Mrs. B said. "I forget what it's called. You don't need an appointment. The girls are nice, and I'm in and out in half an hour." She waited a moment before saying, "Mrs. Oliver? She was Alice's mother?"

Carmella nodded. "Yeah. Oh, they were all afraid of Mrs. Oliver. Nice lady, but the kind you respect, you know what I mean? Not one of these pushover grandmas. Mrs. Oliver held those girls in line. Alice too.

"Of course, she had it tough coming up, Alice did. Her mom was a showgirl in New York. Tall woman, Mrs. Oliver was, even when she was old, and you could tell she used to be beautiful. Wasn't hard to picture her in one of those chorus lines. Truthfully," Carmella dropped her voice, "I don't think Mrs.

Oliver was really Mrs. anything. I don't think she married Alice's dad. I'm not a hundred percent sure, but I got that impression. Nowadays that's no big deal, but you know how it was in our day. That would have been hard on Alice. Mrs. Oliver told me once that Alice's dad was a millionaire but then she stopped talking and never said anything else about him. And she wasn't the type you could ask, so I kept my mouth shut about it. They certainly didn't live like millionaires, though. They didn't have it any better than the rest of us."

The two ladies were rounding the bend toward the Cream King. Myrtle, Anne and Rose were already in line at the little serving window. Mrs. B was in no hurry. The more she knew about Alice, the better.

"She was a good woman, Mrs. Oliver," Carmella said. "Tough on those girls when somebody had to be. It was her that made Jane go to Cassie's christening. Cassie is Tree's daughter. First Tree didn't want to ask Jane to the christening, then her grandmother shamed her into it. Then Jane didn't want to go and her grandmother made her go. She was that kind of lady, Mrs. Oliver. You did what she said.

"I thought she'd have made Tree ask Jane to be in her wedding but I suppose it wouldn't have been right, really, Jane being Greg's old girlfriend and all. Everybody would be talking about Jane at the wedding, and the wedding should be all about the bride, don't you think?"

They made their way down the little slope to the blacktopped parking lot, while a truck roared down the hill toward the bridge. Mrs. B pulled out her change purse.

There were picnic tables next to the Cream King parking lot. The tables and benches were painted red and the paint was only peeling a little. There were trees on the side by the road and, even with the traffic noise, it was really rather pleasant.

Anne, Rose and Myrtle sat down at one of the red tables while Carmella and Mrs. B got in line. Mrs. B got a vanilla cone with sprinkles.

20

A nice breeze periodically ran through the screen door toward the rocking chair in Mrs. B's living room. It felt good. It was quiet tonight on her street, more quiet than usual. Not a lot of cars driving by. Mrs. B had a steaming bowl of beef stew in front of her and there was a charming movie on television. *Apartment for Peggy,* one of her favorites.

There was no reason for Mrs. B to feel anything but content. But that's exactly what she felt. Anything but content.

First, there was that big blue envelope in today's mail. On the front it announced, "The information you requested is inside." She hadn't requested information from anywhere recently, and she almost threw it out unopened, but then decided she might as well see what was inside. A folder full of brochures about Countryside Retirement Village. She threw it in the blue bag she hung on the kitchen door, with all the other paper for recycling, and never gave it another thought until now, when she sat down to eat her supper.

Helen. Helen probably ordered those brochures. What was with that girl?

Mrs. B could remember, clear as day, sitting in this very room, in her old upholstered rocker, singing Polish lullabies as her baby daughter's cries muted to moans and then to the soft, soft breathing on her shoulder. Of course it was true that, as soon as Helen was old enough to talk, the child worried. At first Mrs. B tried to comfort her, but over the years she realized that worrying was her daughter's nature, and no amount of comforting would change that.

She and Albert were so proud when Helen went to college. But from the first day, she began bringing home advice, which Mrs. B politely listened to and mostly ignored. The "improvements" Helen insisted on during her recent visits—the air conditioner, the deadbolt lock on the front door—Mrs. B didn't think they were necessary but they did no harm, and it was fine to let her daughter have her way on those.

But asking her to leave the house she and Albert bought when they were married, the house that for almost all of her life had been her home? That was more than concern, more than advice. It was interference. Helen was treating her mother as if she couldn't take care of herself. Mrs. B could manage her own life very well, thank you.

She took a sip of coffee, then shook her head sadly. Here she was, irritated that she had a daughter who cared too much. Poor Alice has two daughters and neither of them seem to care at all.

There had been times over the years, on rare bad days, when Mrs. B felt sorry for herself because her kids were both so far away. Now that she had seen first-hand the way Alice's daughters talked about their mother, Mrs. B didn't think she'd ever feel sorry for herself again. She was, she decided, extremely fortunate. As annoying as Helen could be, she was the exact opposite of Jane or Tree.

It was difficult to stay angry with Helen when she compared her to the Childers girls. If Mrs. B didn't write to her daughter every week, she knew Helen would call. If she couldn't get her mother on the phone, Helen would call next door to ask Jimmy to check on her. If Jimmy couldn't find Mrs. B and he thought something might be the matter, Helen would call the police. Mrs. B was as sure of that as she was sure there was a God in heaven.

She took a bite of the stew. It was possible, she conceded, that Helen didn't send those brochures. Maybe Mrs. B's name was on a mailing list somewhere because of her age.

Poor, poor Alice. There was no excuse for the way those girls treated their mother.

Though Carmella seemed to think Alice spoiled her girls, Mrs. B knew, even if it was true, that was only a small part of the story. Children go their own way when they reach a certain age. They decide who they're going to be, and they do that all on their own.

Her own family was evidence of that. Mrs. B raised Helen and Leo the same, though of course Leo was allowed a little more leeway, being a boy and a rambunctious one at that. But they got the same amount of love, the same amount of attention. Helen chose college and a career, and Leo chose a darker path. No, not darker really. That's not fair to Leo. A shadowy path, a path that could take him somewhere he couldn't find his way back from. A path where he might, where he *did,* get lost.

Lost. Alice wasn't in the restaurant that day when they went looking for her. They looked everywhere and all around the building. Hopewell was small. It was smaller than Polish Hill, where Mrs. B grew up. If Alice was lost and wandering around Hopewell, someone would have noticed.

Of course, Alice didn't have her wallet. If the police picked up Alice and the poor woman was confused, they wouldn't know who to call.

Was that possible? Could Alice have Alzheimer's? Nobody they'd spoken to gave them any indication that they thought that. Maybe it could come on suddenly. She'd have to remember to ask Dr. Washburn tomorrow when she went for her checkup.

Mrs. B still couldn't believe that Jane Childers lied to that policewoman. You'd think if Jane didn't care to look for her mother she'd at least have the decency to let the officer do her job. Jane Childers wouldn't have the slightest idea if her mother went on a vacation. She didn't even know if her mother had a cell phone.

Nevertheless. As much as she hated to admit it, Jane was right. It really was none of Mrs. B's business. Furthermore, even if Alice wasn't on vacation, there was absolutely no reason to think anything sinister had happened to her.

I've spent my entire life not seeing Alice Childers, Mrs. B thought. All of a sudden I don't see her for a few days and I act like the world turned upside down. There could be a dozen reasons why Alice didn't come to the Senior Center this week. There could be a hundred reasons why she wasn't home when Anne and I stopped by.

But if something is the matter, if something really is the matter, it's my fault. Mine and Anne's. We should have been watching out for her. Kindergarten rules. We shouldn't have come home without her.

But we looked for her. We did. We looked. We were sure she'd gotten a ride with someone else. We wouldn't have come home without her otherwise.

Mrs. B pushed her beef stew away. She had let it get cold.

Eventually, she walked to the kitchen with the bowl of stew and put it in the microwave. She buttered a slice of rye bread while she waited for the little beeps. She needed to quit thinking about this. It wasn't helping, and she should know that. It never helped to think about Leo for too long. She would pray for her son before she went to bed, just like every other night since he'd been gone. She could pray for Alice tonight, too.

By the time she was back in the living room, the movie was almost over. She watched the last scene, then picked up the remote to see if the news was on. Not yet. She sat through an advertisement for those necklaces for old people, where you press a button to call an ambulance. I do have my health, Mrs. B thought. I'm grateful for that.

She went back to the classic movie channel just in time for a listing of three Dorothy McGuire movies they were showing this weekend. Her two favorites, *Claudia* and *The Enchanted Cottage,* would air on Saturday. She made a mental note of it. Then she picked up some stew on her fork, blew on it, and took a bite.

Friday

21

Dr. Washburn looked so concerned, Mrs. B felt a little guilty she'd even asked. He turned from the computer screen to give her his full attention. The big shock of brown hair that surrounded his handsome head partially obscured the laminated chart behind him, the one that detailed with great precision the workings of the human heart. "What happened to make you ask that, Mrs. B?"

"Nothing, Doctor, really. It's just a general question." She was sitting on the edge of the green examination table in the big white office. Her feet swung slowly above the step down to the floor.

Dr. Washburn rolled his little blue stool over to Mrs. B and peered into her eyes like he was searching for the truth. "I've been treating you for a long time now. You know you can trust me."

Mrs. B moved to face him, and the long sheet of white tissue paper rustled underneath her. "I'm fit as a fiddle. That fainting spell was the only problem I had since I saw you last. And that was from the heat."

He nodded. "Yes, you're right this time, it probably was the heat. Those hot spells can be dangerous for someone your age. Nevertheless," he raised his index finger and pointed at her, "I want you to call 9-1-1 if it happens again. Those same symptoms could mean a stroke and, I promise you, if that's the case, you'll be so much better off if it's treated immediately."

"I know that," Mrs. B said. "You told us when you gave that talk at the Senior Center last year."

"Well, listen to me next time. And don't change the subject. Why are you asking me about dementia? What happened?"

"Nothing happened. It's just a general question. I want to be informed. Can Alzheimer's come on suddenly?"

He paused a minute before answering. "I have to preface this by reminding you that's not my field. If something happens, I'll send you to a specialist. But my opinion would be that sudden symptoms of dementia would be more indicative of a stroke."

Mrs. B thought about this for a minute or two while Dr. Washburn sat at the computer with his back to her, typing away. Finally, he stood up. "Josie will have your prescriptions at the front desk. You call me if you have any problems. But as far as I can see, you are right, for someone your age, you're fit as a fiddle. Keep up the walking. It's good for the arthritis in your knee." He reached out his hand to take hers and helped her down from the tall green table.

When Dr. Washburn left the room, Mrs. B made herself presentable while she considered this new information. So, a stroke could cause sudden dementia. It seemed unlikely Alice had a stroke. Don't people fall down when they have a stroke? Someone in the restaurant would have seen that happen. Everyone at Supper Club would have heard about it. Someone would have called for an ambulance. They would have heard the siren, seen the paramedics.

If Alice didn't have dementia, that must mean she didn't wander off. Which left two options. She intentionally left, or someone took her.

Mrs. B considered both while she tied her tennis shoes. Their little yellow flowers were still bright, but the white canvas background was starting to get dingy. She might throw them in the washer when she got home. Or maybe scrub them with a little bleach and a toothbrush.

She picked up her purse, then checked one more time to make sure her blouse was buttoned properly. It's a little too cold in here, she thought as she grabbed the metal door handle. She'd be glad to get outside where it was warmer. The sun would feel good.

It seemed so much more likely, didn't it, that Alice left of her own accord. But where would she have gone? And was she safe there, wherever she was?

22

Mrs. B walked two blocks up the avenue, turned around when she reached the beauty parlor, and headed back toward home. The afternoon sun was hot, and facing this direction it was shining right in her eyes. When she got home she'd put her hat on top of her purse. Then she'd remember to wear it tomorrow. She always seemed to forget, and she had to wonder if it was accidentally on purpose. She didn't like that big brimmed hat she was supposed to wear. When she was a career gal, she always wore a stylish little hat with a feather on it.

Just as Mrs. B reached the pizza shop across from the church, Kelly and Blossom turned the corner.

Spider forged ahead of them, stopping here and there to sniff a telephone pole. Kelly saw her and waved, not just with her hand but with her whole arm. "Hi, Mrs. B!"

Mrs. B waved back as the girls approached. They looked so cute in their pink shorts and purple t-shirts. Both girls wore flip-flops, Kelly's pink, Blossom's yellow. Blossom's thick red hair was caught up on top of her head in a messy ponytail.

"Oh, my gosh, Mrs. B. You won't believe it. Tell her what we saw," Kelly said.

"You tell her," Blossom said.

"Okay, I'll tell her," Kelly said. "We were up Blossom's house."

"Kelly stayed over," Blossom said.

"Yeah, I stayed over. We made brownies but we were only allowed to eat one," Kelly said.

Blossom looked at Kelly and said, "We can have one later."

"Yeah, we can have one later," Kelly said to Mrs. B.

"My mom's strict about brownies," Blossom said to Mrs. B.

Mrs. B headed toward the bench in front of the bus stop. This looked like it could be a long story. The girls followed, one on each side of Mrs. B, with Spider in the lead.

"So, wait till you hear," Kelly said. "You won't believe it. We were walking Spider over by Blossom's house and we walked around the block. That's our new thing we do. We walk around the block."

"We take Spider," Blossom said.

"And then we were walking around this one block up by Blossom's house and then we were walking and walking and then we got to this one house and Spider started barking really loud."

"He hardly ever barks," Blossom said, shaking her head back and forth in emphasis.

"He really doesn't. Hardly ever." Kelly shook her head back and forth too. "But he was barking and barking."

"And then we didn't see anything at that house," Blossom said, "and then Spider started trying to pull us across the street, over to a yellow house."

"So we looked over at the yellow house."

"You won't believe what we saw. You really won't believe it," Blossom said.

Mrs. B sat down on the bench. Spider lay down gently on her feet. She patted him. "What did you see?"

"There was a man's butt sticking out of a window!" Kelly announced.

"It was a cellar window," Blossom said. "You couldn't see his head. All you could see was his pants and big red tennis shoes."

"Just his butt!" Kelly said.

"And then," Blossom said, "the lady next door came out. I thought she was going to yell at us for Spider barking."

"But we pointed and she saw! And then you won't believe it. The lady went and got a big old wiffle bat and started giving the man a licking. For real!" Kelly's eyes were big.

"He was a grownup, too!" Blossom said.

"She hit his butt and started yelling at him and he climbed out and ran across the street. Not by us, up the other way," Kelly said.

"The lady yelled at him the whole time, even when he was running," Blossom said. "She said she was gonna call his mother in Florida and tell on him."

"He could run fast," Kelly said, looking at Blossom. Blossom nodded.

Mrs. B never believed that children should be sheltered. They needed to be prepared to handle things they might encounter in the world. But this worried her. She didn't want these little girls to think of today as a lark. Interrupting a crime in progress was a serious thing. Mrs. B thought about this for a while, petting Spider and scratching him behind the ears. Finally she said, very quietly so they wouldn't know she was worried, "Now you girls know you should always tell a grownup if you see something like that."

"We did!" Blossom said. "We pointed for that lady."

"We stayed across the street the whole time," Kelly said. "We really did, Mrs. B. We just watched the lady give that man a licking." She crouched down next to Spider. "You should have seen it. It was really, really funny."

"The grownups thought it was funny, too. People came out on their porches," Blossom said.

"Spider barked the whole time until the man ran away. Then he stopped barking," Kelly said, rubbing Spider's thick white fur with both her hands.

"I bet that man was afraid of Spider," Blossom said.

"I'll bet he was," Mrs. B said.

"We held Spider so he didn't bite that man's butt. I bet he would have bit that man's butt off if we left go," Kelly said proudly.

They sat quietly for a while, the three of them all petting Spider, who wiggled from the attention.

Finally Mrs. B stood up. "So where are you girls headed?"

"We're walking around this block next," Kelly said. "Want to come?"

Mrs. B smiled. "Thank you, Kelly, but I already had my walk. I'm heading home."

Kelly and Blossom started up the little hill behind the bus stop. Though Burchfield was full of yellow brick houses, the thought nagged at her, and Mrs. B finally asked, her voice raised toward the tops of their heads, "Girls, what street were you on when this happened?"

"Eleanor," Blossom shouted over a bank of hedges.

A yellow house on Eleanor Street. That couldn't be a coincidence.

23

Mrs. B had just settled down on her porch to read the latest issue of *The Guardian* when Anne drove up. Her friend turned down the radio and shouted through the window of her silver sedan, "Did you eat yet?"

Mrs. B shook her head. "No, why?"

"Hop in," Anne said. "We'll go to Eat n' Park."

Mrs. B had to laugh. Honestly, sometimes Anne acted like they were seventeen. Nevertheless, in less than a minute she was locking her front door, purse and sweater over her left arm.

"What prompted this?" Mrs. B asked as she settled into the passenger seat. She had to speak up a little to be heard over Pat Boone, who was singing *April Love* louder than he needed to.

Anne said, "I was watching television and there was an ad for Eat n' Park and I thought, what the heck, why don't I jump in the car and get my supper there. Then when I got in the car I thought, I ought to drive by Ed's and see if she wants to join me."

"I'm glad you did," Mrs. B said. "I heard something interesting today, and it might have something to do with Alice."

Anne turned the radio down. "I can't stop thinking about how nobody's seen that poor woman. I can't believe we left without her. We're terrible people. What if something awful happened to her?"

"We looked everywhere we could think of before we came home on Sunday. We decided someone else must have driven her home, and it made perfect sense at the time." Mrs. B paused. "All the same, I feel guilty, too," she said. "But don't forget, all we know right now is that no one we've talked to has seen her since Sunday afternoon. That's all we know. We don't have a single bit of evidence to suggest anything bad happened."

They were at a stop sign. Anne turned to look at her friend. "You're worried, too."

"Of course I am," Mrs. B said. "But we shouldn't jump to conclusions. We could just be missing each other."

Anne shook her head. "You don't believe that any more than I do. Something is up and you know it. So tell me, what was the interesting thing you heard?"

Mrs. B related her conversation with Kelly and Blossom in detail, Anne nodding but not interrupting as she drove. The restaurant was in nearby Hilltop, and Mrs. B finished her story just as they pulled into the parking lot.

The two ladies walked around to the front of the restaurant. As soon as they entered, Mrs. B put her sweater on. There were quite a few empty tables, and they were quickly seated in a booth. Neither of them looked at the menu.

A dark-haired woman came to their table. She wore a red shirt and a cheerful smile. "What can I get you ladies?"

"Soup and salad bar for me," Anne said.

Mrs. B didn't need to read the woman's name tag. Their waitress was the girl Leo took to St. Mary's junior prom. "Same for me, Susie. And a cup of decaf coffee."

"Decaf for me, too, please," Anne said.

Steam rose from the metal cauldron as Mrs. B ladled chicken noodle soup into a cool white bowl.

By the time she'd set it on their table and slid into the caramel-colored bench, Anne was already crumbling crackers into a bowl of chili. Anne looked up and said, "I think I know what he was looking for."

"Who?"

"Alice's burglar."

"We don't know for sure it was Alice's house," Mrs. B said.

Anne gave her a look.

Mrs. B blew on a spoonful of soup. "Okay, let's assume it was. What was he looking for?"

"Apparently it's common knowledge at the crafts table that Alice's mother was a chorus girl in New York."

"I heard that, too," Mrs. B said. "Carmella told me the other day."

"Did she tell you about all the trouble between Alice and her girls when their grandmother died?"

Mrs. B said, "She told me their grandmother was the one who held the family together."

Anne said, "It's more than that. Alice's grandmother had an emerald necklace."

Mrs. B had a little ruby pendant in her jewelry box, a long-ago gift from Albert. It certainly wasn't worth fighting over. "What kind of emerald necklace?"

"Alice's father gave it to her. The girls at the crafts table said he was a Rockefeller or a Mellon or somebody like that. Maybe it was a Vanderbilt." She paused for a second, then shook her head. "I don't know, some millionaire." She paused, then looked at Mrs. B. "Do you think that could be true?"

"It's not impossible," Mrs. B said. "Especially if her mother was a beautiful chorus girl in New York."

"I don't know," Anne said. "Alice doesn't live any better than the rest of us. Why would she live in Burchfield if her father was a Vanderbilt?"

Mrs. B opened her saltine crackers and bit into one. Then she said, "Carmella said Alice's mother's name was Mrs. Oliver."

"I never heard of any rich Olivers," Anne said.

Mrs. B stirred her soup and took another spoonful.

"Oh!" Anne said finally, lowering her voice. "Do you think Alice was illegitimate?"

"Things do seem to point in that direction," Mrs. B said.

"Alice's mom wouldn't have made a stink about it. Not like they do now, letting everyone know they had an affair. She'd keep that sort of thing a secret," Anne said.

Mrs. B nodded her head ever so slightly. "She'd worry about Alice's reputation as well as her own.

She wouldn't want anyone to know she had a daughter born out of wedlock."

"Maybe they were star-crossed lovers. And the emerald necklace, that might be the only thing Mrs. Oliver had to remember the man she loved. That would explain why she didn't sell it."

Mrs. B nodded, then looked at Anne. "Remember, we're just speculating. This is starting to sound more like a movie than real life."

"You're always telling me that truth is stranger than fiction," Anne said.

"I do say that, don't I?" Mrs. B looked down at her empty bowl. "Let's go get our salads."

Mrs. B picked up one of the cold clear plates and made her way down the salad bar. Lettuce, cucumbers, mushrooms, little tomatoes. Olives, beets, cottage cheese. She decided against the bread but on the way back to her table added one of the cute little blueberry muffins.

Anne's plate of greenery was topped with sliced peaches. She put one on her fork and wiggled it as she continued. "Well, here's what I heard today. When their grandmother died, Jane and Tree both told Alice they wanted the emerald necklace and Alice wouldn't give it to them."

Mrs. B took a bite of a cucumber, chewing as she thought. "If we're right, of course Alice would want to keep the necklace. It might be her only connection to her father."

They ate their salads in silence for a while. Finally Mrs. B said, "I hate to say it, but I don't like those girls one bit."

"They're not America's sweethearts, are they?" Anne said.

"Sometimes I worry that we're overreacting, but something could really be the matter," Mrs. B said. "Someone needs to be worrying about Alice. It's hard to believe her daughters could be so completely unconcerned when no one has seen their mother for days."

"If my friends couldn't find me and they told my daughters, those girls would cause so much commotion," Anne said.

"If Helen calls and leaves a message for me and I don't call her back that day, she calls next door to find out if Jimmy's seen me. I much prefer when we write letters. I never think to look to see if I have phone messages." Mrs. B speared a tomato with her fork, then set it down. "Alice doesn't have anybody to worry about her."

"She has us," Anne said.

"She does," Mrs. B said. "She has us." She ate the tomato, then reached into her purse and put a pencil and a little notebook on the table.

"What's that for?" Anne said.

"I'll tell you later," Mrs. B said, "when we're done eating."

24

After Susie had poured their third cup of coffee and come back with more cream, Mrs. B picked up her #2 pencil and said, "Let's make a list of places Alice could be."

Anne thought for a minute. "Something could have happened to her."

"Okay, what would that something be?"

"Someone murdered her."

"Now why would they do that?" Mrs. B asked.

"Maybe they tried to rob her and she fought back."

"She didn't even have her purse. It was in your trunk, remember?"

"Jane or Tree might have murdered her."

"Be serious."

"I'm dead serious. Both of them want that necklace."

"It's a big jump from wanting a necklace to killing your mother."

Anne just looked at her.

Mrs. B said, "You watch too many crime dramas."

"Maybe someone kidnapped her," Anne said.

Mrs. B thought about it for a minute. "I don't know. Why on earth would someone kidnap Alice? Who would they call for ransom? Certainly not her daughters."

"Not if they knew them," Anne said. "Good point." She stirred sweetener into her coffee. "She could have wandered off somewhere. Like that girl's aunt at the little store where we got the popsicles."

Mrs. B shook her head. "I asked Dr. Washburn about that. He said loss of memory doesn't come out of nowhere. He said the only thing he could think of that would make that happen is if she had a stroke."

"If Alice had a stroke she would have fallen down," Anne said. "One of us would have seen her. Or someone in the restaurant would have. And we walked all through that place, and all around the outside."

"I don't think that's it," Mrs. B said. "But let's not rule it out."

She wrote 'memory loss' on the list, then put the pencil down and took another sip of her coffee. "Now, she might have wandered off on her own accord."

"And gotten involved in something and missed us," Anne said. "Do you think she went to the county fair?"

"That's possible," Mrs. B said. "It would be a very impulsive thing to do, though."

"She didn't have a way home," Anne said. "Not that we know of, anyhow. And why wouldn't she be at the Senior Center the next day?"

"And why wouldn't she be home? No, I don't think she went to the county fair. Not without her purse." Mrs. B absently reached toward the little metal rack at the end of the table and pulled out the dessert menu. There was a slice of strawberry pie on the cover. "Maybe she did come home, though. Maybe we just keep missing her."

"I don't think she's been home. Her neighbor next door that we talked to, she would have seen her."

"Probably, but let's not rule it out." She wrote it down, then looked at the notebook. "Wait, that doesn't make sense. If she was home, why wouldn't she try to find you so she could get her purse?" She flipped the pencil to the eraser end.

Anne said, "Maybe we made her mad somehow and she doesn't want to talk to us."

"There was fifteen dollars in her purse," Mrs. B said. "She'd have to be fifteen dollars worth of mad. And we didn't do anything to make her mad."

"Maybe somebody else drove her home later and she was mad we didn't wait for her."

"That would make sense. But why haven't we seen her at the Senior Center all week, or why hasn't she been home?"

"Some people are very sensitive. Maybe we hurt her feelings. Maybe she pretends she isn't home when she sees us," Anne said.

"That's possible. She doesn't seem like the type, from what everyone says, but we don't really know her ourselves. Not well, anyway." Mrs. B opened the dessert menu between them so they could both see it. "We didn't even talk to Alice much. We couldn't hear each other riding out to the country in the convertible, and then when we got there she didn't sit with us. She sat with Old Mike and Carmella, remember?"

"Hmm," Anne said. She tilted her head, thinking. "Maybe it wasn't even us she got mad at. Maybe someone else made her mad, and she doesn't want to talk to any of us, and that's why she hasn't come to the Senior Center."

"Some people are like that. We can't rule it out. Maybe you're right. Maybe she really was home when we came by. Maybe she hid when she saw us coming." She picked up the pencil and added "home" back to the list. "I hope it's that simple, but I don't think that's it. If she was home, she would want her purse back."

"Probably," Anne said. She put the dessert menu back in its little metal holder. "I don't know why we're looking at this. We both know we're getting strawberry pie."

Mrs. B nodded absentmindedly, her eyes still on the notebook. "So we have 'memory loss' and 'home'. What else? Be serious. Something that actually might have happened, not something you saw last night on TV."

"Maybe she fell in love with someone at first sight and they eloped," Anne said.

"Now you're just being silly," Mrs. B said.

"Let's talk about this man climbing in the window. That can't be a coincidence," Anne said.

"No, I'm sure you're right there. That has to figure in here somehow."

Susie came by again, orange-handled coffeepot in hand. "Dessert, ladies?"

"Strawberry pie," Anne said.

"Make that two," Mrs. B said.

"Now that's a whole different angle," Mrs. B said as soon as the waitress left. "What we need to know is, does this emerald necklace exist? And who tried to break into Alice's house? If it really was Alice's house."

"It was Alice's house," Anne said. "I bet you a dollar."

Mrs. B thought about it. "No bet. I'm sure you're right. It's too much of a coincidence. So," she said, picking up the pencil again, "who climbed in the window?"

"It could have been just a regular ordinary burglar."

"Doesn't that seem awfully coincidental?"

"Maybe the burglar is someone who lives nearby and noticed Alice hasn't been home since Sunday."

"That could be." Mrs. B wrote 'ordinary burglary' in the notebook. "But it could also be that someone was after the necklace. If it does indeed exist." She thought for a moment. "Or even if someone thinks it does."

Anne looked up from her coffee. "Jane's boyfriend or Tree's husband, that's what I think. One of those two."

"They do seem likely candidates," Mrs. B said. "But don't forget, this is Burchfield. Half the people in town probably know about that necklace. You found out at the crafts table."

Anne nodded. "Almost everybody already knew about it."

"We're basing this all on a rumor," Mrs. B said. "We don't even truly know if the necklace exists." She tapped her pencil on the table, thinking. Finally she looked up. "Did any of the crafts ladies describe the necklace? Had they ever seen it?"

Anne thought, then said, "No. If someone described it I would have a picture of it in my head. And I don't."

"Well, there you see," Mrs. B said. "We don't even know if there is a necklace."

"We do know someone tried to climb in a window on her street," Anne said.

Mrs. B nodded. "And it's a fair bet it was Alice's house."

Anne waved to a grey-haired lady in a pink sweater who was sitting a few booths away, then turned back to Mrs. B. "Oh, the other thing I learned today. Jane's boyfriend is quite a bit younger than her. His name is Nicky. The house they live in belongs to his parents. Jane moved in there after the parents moved away."

"Who are his parents, do you know?" Mrs. B said.

"No," Anne said, "Nobody said anything about them, just that they moved. His parents would be younger than us. Maybe they were new people."

Mrs. B knew what "new people" meant in Burchfield. She had had been in Burchfield for all these decades, yet some people still considered her a "new person" because she hadn't grown up there. "That's a possibility," she said.

Virginia, the woman in the pink sweater, came toward their booth just then, purse on her arm, wallet and check in her hand. Years ago, when Mrs. B volunteered at St. Mary's School library, Virginia had been the sixth grade teacher. Mrs. B closed her notebook and tucked it back into her purse.

"Well, hello! Ed, it's been so long, it's good to see you," Virginia said.

After their greetings, Mrs. B said, "Virginia, this is going to sound like a question from out of the blue, but were Mary Jane and Theresa Childers in your sixth grade, or were they in Sister Imelda's?

Virginia rolled her eyes. "That was those two Protestant girls. Their grandmother sent them to St. Mary's, and I always figured it was because of the way they acted up. Thought the nuns might be able to straighten them out. Those girls were in my class, both of them. That Mary Jane, she was a piece of work. Butter wouldn't melt in her mouth, that one. She'd look you straight in the eye and lie to you. I remember a time I saw her pass a note, *saw* her pass it, and she swore to me she hadn't. Swore it up and down, like she thought I was delusional.

"Theresa was a bit of a hooligan, but at least with her you knew what you were getting. Even when she was defiant she wouldn't lie, even if it would do her good. Of course, I did my best to be understanding, their father dying so young. But those girls tried me, both of them." She shook her head. "What on earth brought them up?"

Mrs. B looked at Anne, and Anne said, "Alice Childers started coming to the Senior Center. It made us think about her girls, wonder what they're doing now."

Virginia said, "They're both still in Burchfield, I know that. Mary Jane lives up on the hill, in the Cibulka's house. She started dating little Nicky Cibulka after his parents moved to Tampa. He's only a boy, I bet he just turned 25. Middle-aged women dating young men. I don't understand that at all. What on earth do they talk about?"

Anne winked. "Maybe there's not a lot of conversation."

"Oh, Anne, you're wicked," Virginia said, laughing.

As Virginia headed to the front counter to pay her check, Mrs. B turned to Anne. "Jane's boyfriend's parents live in Florida. Kelly and her friend said the burglar's parents live in Florida. That had to be Alice's house."

Susie placed a slice of strawberry pie in front of each of the ladies. Both were piled high with whipped cream. Mrs. B put a strawberry on her fork and dipped it in the whipped cream, then looked at Anne. "What are you doing tomorrow?"

Anne already had a forkful of pie in her mouth. "What's tomorrow, Saturday? I have to take my books back to the library, that's all. Why? Are you thinking what I'm thinking?"

Mrs. B nodded just as Susie came back with more coffee. "We need to go up to Eleanor Street again. And bring Alice's purse with you. There might be a clue in there."

25

Mrs. B set the book upside down in her lap, folded open to her page. She reached for her lemonade. Water beaded on the glass. She took a sip, set it back on the porch rail and wiped her wet hand on the leg of her pink slacks.

Kelly waved from across the street. Mrs. B waved back. There were two little girls with Kelly this time. One was Blossom, but there was another. Taller. A little older, maybe.

Mrs. B started to pick up her book again, but then she saw the girls headed down Kelly's steps. Kelly and Blossom looked both ways, crossed the street, and then bounded onto Mrs. B's porch, the taller girl trailing behind.

"This is Cassie," Kelly said, presenting the girl as if she were a prize on a game show. "She lives by Blossom."

From close up, Mrs. B could see that Cassie was maybe a year or two older than Kelly, and a few inches taller. The girl's lanky frame sported green shorts and a light blue t-shirt decorated with faded glittery stars. Her short hair was dishwater blonde and her eyes were pale green, big and round. She looked at Mrs. B, then shyly at the porch's cement floor. "Hi," she said, so quietly Mrs. B could hardly hear her.

The child's face, her halting voice, clutched at Mrs. B's heart. Alice's granddaughter, she had to be. This was the girl they saw on Tree's porch, carrying the watermelon. "Hi, honey," Mrs. B said.

Cassie stood on the front porch next to Mrs. B's white wooden rocker. Kelly and Blossom stood on the steps, watching. Kelly leaned against the railing and stood on one foot, dangling the other over the step below. She said, "Cassie wants to talk to you. We told her you were the lady on her porch. Remember that time you went over Cassie's house and we saw you but we didn't say hi?"

"I told Cassie she could come and see you," Blossom chimed in proudly, her red curls bouncing. "I told her you were nice."

"Well, thank you, Blossom," Mrs. B said. She turned toward Cassie and said in her gentlest voice, "Honey, is there something you want to talk to me about?"

Cassie rubbed the toe of a blue flip-flop on the cement. "Remember when you were on our porch talking to my mom?" she said, taking her time over each word. "I was in the living room. I could hear you." She paused as if she wasn't sure what to say next. "Sorry she yelled at you. She does that. She yells at people. A lot." Cassie paused again, then stood straighter and taller, as if she'd summoned up courage. "Did something happen to my grandma?" she asked. "Is my grandma all right?"

Mrs. B thought for a moment before she responded. She didn't want to alarm the girl, but she didn't want to lie to her, either. She said, "I haven't seen your grandma for a few days, honey, so I've been looking for her."

Cassie looked straight into Mrs. B's eyes. "Did something bad happen?"

Poor child. How should she explain this? "I was looking for your grandma and I couldn't find her.

She wasn't at home, and your mother and your Aunt Jane didn't know where she was." Mrs. B reached for the little girl's hand. "So I'm still looking for her, and as soon as I find her, I'll tell Kelly. And Kelly can let you know."

Cassie's eyes were moist with tears. She said, "I love my grandma."

"Of course you do, honey," Mrs. B said, patting her hand. "Of course you do. I promise, I'll let Kelly know as soon as I find her."

"Mrs. B can find your grandma, even if nobody else can," Kelly said. "She's so smart. You wouldn't believe how many books she reads."

26

When Mrs. B came inside, she put her empty lemonade glass into the sink and picked up her #2 pencil to take another stab at the crossword puzzle. On her way to the living room, the hallway seemed dim compared to the light outside. Just as she walked by the phone, it rang, and she picked it up on the first ring. The white plastic was cool on her ear.

"Mom, thank goodness!" There was a pause. Then Helen said, "Why didn't you answer the phone?"

"I just did. It just rang," Mrs. B said.

"I tried three times to call you."

Mrs. B glanced down at the phone with its big white buttons. The answering machine's little red light was blinking. "Why, honey, is something the matter?"

Helen's voice was sharp. "Mama, where were you?"

Mrs. B noticed she still had the yellow pencil in her hand. She set it down next to the phone. "I went out with a friend and got something to eat. Then I sat on the porch and read for a while. I guess I didn't hear the phone ring. Why, what's going on?"

"I called to see how your doctor appointment went. It was today, wasn't it? And when I couldn't get you on the phone…"

"For goodness sake, honey, I just went up to Eat n' Park. Here, hold on a minute." She dragged a chair from the kitchen table into the hallway, then sat down and picked up the phone again. "Okay, I'm back."

Her daughter's voice was softer now. "I didn't know what to do when you weren't home, Mom. You didn't tell me you'd planned an evening out."

"Why would you have to do anything, honey? Just wait for me to come home."

"I didn't know what happened. After that whole thing about you fainting…" Helen's voice drifted off.

"Honey, I can't tell you everything I'm doing every day of the week," Mrs. B said. "If I'm not here, you need to assume everything's fine. If something's the matter, I promise I'll have someone call you."

Neither of them said anything for a while. A car door slammed outside, and Mrs. B heard someone hollering over to someone else. Then a dog started to bark. Eventually Helen asked, "What happened at the doctor's?"

Mrs. B reached into her pocket and heard something crinkle. She said, "Nothing, really. It was just a checkup."

"What about the fainting?"

Mrs. B pulled her hand out of her pocket. She was clutching a little round disk of red-and-white-striped peppermint candy. "He said it was probably the heat."

Helen's voice went up an octave. "Probably? He isn't going to take tests or anything?"

Mrs. B twisted the cellophane around the candy to open it. "Dr. Washburn knows what he's doing. He's treated me for years, and I'm still around to tell about it." There was a sputtery noise outside. She looked out the hallway window. Next door, Jimmy was washing down his back porch with the hose.

Helen started again. "Mom, you can't just..."

Mrs. B interrupted. "Honey, you've got to stop getting yourself all worked up. It's not good for you."

Her daughter's voice came back clipped and sharp. "Honestly, Mama, there's no talking to you sometimes."

Mrs. B picked up her pencil and bounced it, eraser first, on the little telephone table. The two of them spent another few minutes on idle chatter until Mrs. B asked wasn't it late out there, what time was it in London, and Helen said you know darn well what time it is here and they both decided they'd had enough of each other for the night and the two of them hung up.

Mrs. B replaced the receiver with one hand and popped the peppermint into her mouth with the other. She dragged the chair back to the kitchen, then poured a mug of cold coffee and stuck it in the microwave. When it was warm, she picked up her pencil again and took the crossword puzzle to the living room.

Saturday

27

Mrs. B's coffeemaker gurgled as it finished brewing the morning pot of coffee. The milk was already on the kitchen table, along with a loaf of raisin bread and a block of cream cheese. Mrs. B walked toward the coffeemaker, two rose-colored mugs in hand.

The bread popped up. Anne took it out of the toaster, then wiggled her fingers. "Ooh, that's hot!" She put toast on two plates, then sat down and pulled a packet of sweetener out of her pocket. She shook it, then tore it open and poured half of it in her mug and gave it a stir. She folded the packet over and stuck it back in her pocket.

Mrs. B blew on her coffee and took a sip while Anne cut a chunk of the cream cheese and began to spread it on her toast. Anne said, "The color of these mugs is exactly the same as the flowers on your tablecloth."

Mrs. B compared them. "I never noticed before. Helen got me these when she was out here at Eastertime." She took a bite of her toast. "So, is your daughter still mad at you for driving the convertible?"

"Oh, she's always mad at me for something. Don't think a week's gone by this summer that wasn't the case."

"Helen's mad at me," Mrs. B said.

Anne reached for a smidgen more of cream cheese. "What'd you do now?"

"She wants me to move into one of those retirement homes."

"What for?"

Mrs. B nodded. "That's what I said."

After breakfast, they went into the living room for the serious business of the morning—going through Alice's purse again, looking for any sort of clue that might tell them where she was.

Anne sat on the loveseat and poured the contents of the purse onto the coffee table. The pack of breath mints rolled out and she caught them before they hit the floor. "Hey, want to go for a drive tomorrow? I want to see if Sarris Candies has any Sen-Sen."

Mrs. B was peering through the screen door. She nodded. "That sounds nice."

Anne said, "Bring your babushka. We'll take the convertible."

Mrs. B turned toward Anne. "You know, Alice's granddaughter came over here yesterday after you dropped me off. Sweet little thing."

"What?" Anne said. "Why didn't you tell me before? What did she say?"

"She's worried. She overheard us all talking when we were up there," Mrs. B said.

"Oh, no," Anne said. "We probably scared the child. Guess she's not tough like her mother."

"She must take after her father," Mrs. B said. "She was shy."

"So what did you tell her?"

Mrs. B crossed the room and sat next to her friend. "What could I say? I told her we'd keep looking for her grandma, and we'd let her know when we found her. You should have seen the little girl, Anne. I can't get her face out of my mind."

Almost absentmindedly, Mrs. B picked up the change purse from the coffee table and emptied it into the palm of her hand. Thirty-two cents. Two dimes, a nickel and seven pennies. Nothing else. She put the coins back and reached for the wallet.

A ten and a five. Pictures of Tree and Jane. Voter's registration. A punch card from a nearby nursery—buy 12 plants, get one free. Six punches so far.

Anne said, "I guess she doesn't take the bus much, or else she'd have her Medicare card in here."

"It's pretty far from her house to the bus stop," Mrs. B said.

Nothing inside the little package of tissues. The lip balm was regular lip balm. Cherry flavored. The mints were only mints.

"Not much here," Mrs. B said.

"You wouldn't take much if you were just going to supper."

"That's true." Mrs. B picked up the little coin purse and held it in her hand, thinking. She opened it again, dumped the coins into her palm. She looked at each one separately, turning it over and over. She ran her fingers through the inside of the little empty purse, then put the coins back and reached for the wallet. Again, everything out, one by one. Each photo, each card from its little plastic sleeve. Nothing behind any of them. She turned each over and over before she put it back. She took the bills from the wallet and ran her fingers through the fold, looking for a secret pocket, but there wasn't one. It was just an ordinary wallet filled with ordinary things.

She picked up the purse itself and turned it inside out as far as it would go. She shook it. Nothing rattled, nothing fell out. As she went to put it right again, she ran her fingers along the top of the purse and she saw it. A tiny zipper, the same color as the lining. She opened it and reached inside. Slowly, she pulled out a house key and held it up for Anne to see.

Anne looked grave. "No matter how mad you were at someone, you would still want your house key."

Mrs. B nodded. "We need to call the police," she said.

Anne pursed her lips. "Yeah, they were a lot of help."

Mrs. B put the key back in the little pocket. "You're right. They can't do anything about it when Alice's daughters say otherwise."

The two of them sat in silence. Outside there was a humming sound. Probably a lawn mower. Mrs. B looked at the clock. Midmorning. Yes, probably a lawn mower. Or a hedge cutter. People doing their Saturday chores.

A dog barked. A couple of cars went by. Finally, Mrs. B stood up. "We need to go back up to Alice's house."

Anne stuffed the contents back into Alice's purse and threw it over her arm as Mrs. B shut off the coffeemaker and went to the front door, her own key in hand.

28

The lilies in front of Alice's house glistened, and the sprinkler was wet. "Looks like the garden was watered. She must be home," Anne said.

"That'll be a relief," Mrs. B said.

They knocked. No answer. They walked around to the kitchen. On the way, Mrs. B looked at the hose. There was a white dial attached to it. She looked closer. "Sprinkler's on a timer," she said.

The kitchen was dark and quiet. They went back to the front of the house and Mrs. B looked through the mail slot. A stack of mail sat on Alice's living room floor.

"Let's go knock next door," Mrs. B said.

"Oh, good idea. I want to ask her if she knows anything about the guy climbing in the window."

They crossed the pavement to the porch at the next house. Through the screen door they could see the woman they'd seen on Tuesday. She wore blue jeans, a big red t-shirt that hung almost to her knees, and bedroom slippers. The t-shirt had a picture of three cats snuggled up on a pillow. The woman was talking on the phone. "Listen, I gotta go. Someone's at the door. Someone's at the door. I gotta go. Yeah, I'll call you back." She turned to the ladies. "You still looking for Alice?"

They nodded.

"I don't know where she is. Not like her to just up and take off."

Mrs. B said, "There's a stack of mail on the floor in her living room. I looked through the slot."

The woman walked into her kitchen and came back with a key, talking the whole time. "She usually tells me if she's gonna be away so I can watch the house. Not that she goes away much. Two years ago she went to see her cousin in Chicago. Took the train. She likes to be home, though. In the summer she always putzes around in her garden. She only went to Chicago that time because there was a funeral. She usually stays home." She looked at Anne. "You're Cathy's mom, right?"

Anne said, "You know my Cathy?"

"I'm Patty. I used to bartend down at the Grill. She came in Friday nights for a fish sandwich. Her and her guy. This was before she was married."

"That was probably when she was with Ralph."

Patty walked toward Alice's house, Anne and Mrs. B trailing behind her. "No, his name wasn't Ralph." She stopped and thought for a second. "Teddy."

Anne said, "Oh, I remember a Teddy. That was a while ago."

"Yeah, it's been a while. You came in once and had a drink with them. She introduced us."

"I'm sorry I don't remember," Anne said.

"Oh, that's okay. I'm one of those people that remembers faces." Patty pushed open the front door and started picking up the mail. Mrs. B braced herself for the worst as they walked through the door, but the house was quiet and serene.

"Smells like peaches in here," Anne said.

"Room freshener," Patty said, nodding toward a tiny glass jar plugged into the wall.

Anne said, "We heard someone tried to break into a house on your street the other day."

"Boy, that's Burchfield for you. News travels, don't it." Patty put the mail in a neat pile on Alice's kitchen counter. "That was that jagoff Nicky, Mary Jane's boyfriend. *Boyfriend,*" she said derisively. "Don't know why she wants to be with a boy half her age." She darted a look at Anne. "Shouldn't say that. I know why. Just think she should know better." She nodded toward the side of the house. "He was trying to get in here. I chased him out. Jagoff."

Patty kept the monologue going as she opened the cellar door and turned on the light. "Alice, you down here?" she shouted, then walked down the steps. Mrs. B peered after her. There was a bookcase at the end of the steps. In front of it, on the cement floor, was an old red shop-vac. Patty turned to the right and disappeared for a moment, then appeared again and climbed back to the kitchen. She shut off the light and turned back to Anne. "Locked that window. Should have checked on Alice, I guess, after Nicky trying to climb in her window. But just when I was getting ready to knock on her door, my calico jumped out the window and hid under the Runco's porch. I can't leave her outside like that, had to climb under there after her. She's declawed. Then I was covered in cobwebs and ended up having to change my clothes and go take a shower. Forgot all about checking on Alice. I should have checked on her."

Patty washed her hands in Alice's kitchen sink, then dried them on a yellow dish towel hanging near the refrigerator. On the front of the fridge, held by a yellow banana magnet, was a child's crayon drawing of a rainbow. It was curled at the edges and bleached on one side, probably from the sun coming in through the kitchen window. "Alice used to be out all the time when she had Maizie. Walked her all the way down to the ballfield most days. Little Maizie, cute little mongrel. Didn't like my cats, though. I think she was afraid of my Siamese. My Siamese is old but she's feisty. Poor Alice was so upset when she had to put Maizie down. They're part of your family, aren't they? She didn't have nobody with Maizie gone. Her kids aren't good for nothing. She ought to get another dog. I understand she might not want to get one right away. But a dog is good for someone like Alice, alone like that. Gets her out of the house."

Patty headed toward the upstairs. They heard her walking around but she came right back down the steps, shaking her head. "She's not home. She must have gone somewhere and not told me. That's weird."

Mrs. B asked, "Does Alice have any other family around here, besides her girls?"

"Nope, not since her mom died."

Anne said, "What about outside the city, toward Hopewell?"

"I don't even know where that is," Patty said. "Anyhow, she don't have nobody. Not since her mom died. Just those two girls, and they aren't good for nothing. She's got people in Chicago, like I said, but that's all I ever heard of. Guess there maybe could have been another funeral. But she would have come over to ask me to watch the house. I'd have probably drove her to the train station."

Patty started to roam around the downstairs, and Mrs. B and Anne followed. The house was neat as a pin. Mrs. B wandered over to the bookshelf. It was full of paperbacks, all of them romances. "People usually give those away, or trade them," Patty said. "That's what I do with mine. Alice will trade me once in a while. She used to trade with Carmella a lot. Do you know Carmella? She goes to the Senior Center. But Alice keeps a lot of hers. The ones she likes, she reads them again and again. She reads a lot. Usually out on her porch in the summertime. Now that I think of it, I haven't seen her out all week. I should have looked for her, I guess. Especially with Nicky climbing in her window like that."

The magazine rack in the living room was filled with gardening magazines. Anne leafed through them, then picked one up and read the title. "Mother Earth News. Never saw this one."

Mrs. B said, "I've seen that at the library. It's for people who practice self-reliance. Tells you how to build a fence, how to raise organic vegetables, things like that."

"Oh, that sounds like Alice," Patty said as she pointed to the bench next to the gardening boots. "She built that, all by herself. Learned how to do that sort of thing after her old man died. Really took to it. She has a workshop down the cellar, just like a guy. Bookshelf down there, too, books and magazines. Popular Mechanics, stuff like that." She started rooting through the umbrella stand behind the boots.

"My son used to read that one," Mrs. B said.

"Mine, too," Anne said. "I didn't know it was still around."

Patty went to the kitchen window and pointed to a little rock fountain along the backyard fence. She said, "Yeah, I think that's how she learned how to make that fountain. One of those magazines."

"She made that herself?" Anne said.

"Yeah, put in her own garbage disposal, too. Those no-good daughters of hers don't send their men over to help her out, the way they should. Course Greg comes over once in a while to check up on her. Tree's husband. Probably has to tell Tree he's going out for cigarettes and then sneak over. Don't know how he can live with that girl. He's a good guy, though, Greg is. Always says hi to me when he's over here."

On top of the television in the living room there was a large photo in a wooden frame, a picture of Alice in her backyard, holding her granddaughter's hand. Mrs. B picked it up and looked at it. "I took that," Patty said. "Turned out nice, didn't it? You can see all the flowers. That's a few years ago. Cassie was maybe five or six. I think she just was starting school when I took that."

Mrs. B set it back on the television. "Does Alice own an expensive necklace?"

"Yeah, that's no secret. Belonged to her mom."

"Do you know where she keeps it?"

"No, but we should probably look for that. Don't want Nicky Cibulka walking off with it. Alice told me she has it put away but she never said where. You check down here. Me and Cathy's mom will go upstairs."

Mrs. B stood for a moment in each room, thinking of likely hiding places. In the living room she looked behind the books in the bookcase and under the couch cushions. In the kitchen she stuck a long spoon into the flour canister. Nothing there. She rinsed off the spoon and put it in the dish rack. She checked the freezer. There was a blue plastic container with $40 in it, but no necklace.

Anne and Patty came back down the stairs. "Did you find it?" Patty asked. Mrs. B shook her head.

"Well, if we can't find it, Nicky won't be able to either. He's not real bright. You ladies want to come over for coffee? I put a pot on right before you came."

29

Patty's kitchen was painted white. Red and white curtains framed a window that looked out into the backyard, and a wallpaper border of black and white cats rimmed the ceiling. A fluffy calico sat in Patty's lap and she petted it as she talked.

"Alice was always trying to be a good mom but she was too nice, you know how some people are too nice, and they always took advantage of her. Then when Gladys died and Alice wouldn't give the girls that necklace… Do you need sugar?"

Mrs. B was pouring milk into her coffee. She shook her head. Anne had already reached into her pocket and was pouring the other half of the sweetener packet into her cup.

"I saw the necklace once, when Gladys, Alice's mom, was still alive. She wore it to Cassie's christening party with a pale green dress. It was gorgeous, like something out of the movies. There were so many emeralds." She paused, then said, "That had to be what Nicky was after, that snake.

"You know, those girls weren't always so awful. I babysat for them sometimes when they were little, when the grownups went dancing down the Legion Hall. They behaved for me. It was after their dad died they got like they are now. Alice spoiled them, gave in to them all the time. Course she was always like that. It was their dad laid down the law. And Gladys, nobody messed with Gladys.

"Wonder where Alice went without telling me? Maybe something came up real quick. If it was on a Thursday I might have been at bingo."

"We haven't seen her since Sunday," Anne said.

"Well, Alice isn't one to tell everyone her business. She keeps herself to herself, as far as I can see, even with me. I was always the one to come over the house and say hey, let's have a cup of iced tea and sit on the porch, or hey, I got a bushel of apples, let's make pie. Alice makes really good pie crust. I always do the insides part.

"When she had Maizie I used to see her all the time cause she'd be out walking Maizie. Maizie died a couple of weeks ago. That's when I talked Alice into going to the Senior Center. After Maizie died. Alice didn't want to go, she thought it was just for the Catholics and she goes to the Presbyterian church. Well, really, I don't think she's gone since her girls grew up, but that's where she used to go. I told her Charlie down the street and his wife, they go to the Senior Center, and they go to Third Baptist down in Rockwood. So that's how I talked her into it."

The calico wriggled and Patty put it on the kitchen floor. It rubbed against Anne's leg and she scratched its fur.

"I can't be the only person Alice talks to," Patty said. "That's not good for her. Cassie used to come over once in a blue moon, but she had to hide it from her mom. Isn't that awful? I don't think Cassie's been here for a while. Probably got caught and got a licking."

Mrs. B shook her head sadly.

Patty said, "I got my own kids and my grandkids and my nieces and nephews and I don't have time to keep Alice company every day even if I wanted to. I guess she could have knocked on my door to ask me to watch the house, but I don't think I was home Sunday. Sunday was the night it rained so hard, right? I was at my nephew's for supper. We were watching that show, not CSI, the other one, anyhow there was this lady, her kids kept saying she went on vacation but really they killed her and put her in a garbage bag and dropped her in the ocean. It was raining that day, too, on the show. At least we know that didn't happen to Alice. Her ungrateful little bitches aren't smart enough do something like that. Anyhow, neither of them has a boat."

Patty drank some coffee, then shook her head. "I shouldn't have said that, I guess. Shouldn't talk like that, even for a joke. Tree and Mary Jane, they're disrespectful, and Tree's got a temper, had that even when she was a kid and it sure didn't get any better, and that Mary Jane, she takes up with a boy half her age so we know she don't got much sense. Though like I said I know why," she looked at Anne and Mrs. B knowingly, "but that still don't mean she has any sense. And she lies like a rug. But I know deep down those girls have to love their mother. They're greedy and selfish, but they have to love their mother. That's their *mother*."

Mrs. B had just finished off the last bit of coffee in her cup when the phone rang. Patty looked over at it, then said, "My sister and her daughter are fighting over where they're having the grandbaby's birthday. First the niece calls me, now it's my sister." Patty picked up the phone. Mrs. B and Anne put their cups in the sink and waved as they walked out. Patty waved back, still talking.

As they walked toward the car, Mrs. B said, "Let's get that key out of Alice's purse. I want to borrow that picture of her on top of the TV. We might want that later."

30

When Mrs. B got home, she opened the front door really wide to cool off the living room. On her way to the kitchen, she noticed the red light blinking on her answering machine.

"Mom, I guess you're out shopping or something. I'll call again in a little while. I need your advice on something."

Well, that's a nice change of pace, Mrs. B thought. Maybe Helen's mood had softened since yesterday.

She dragged a chair from the kitchen to the hall-way and put it next to the phone. Then she pulled a can of lemonade out of the freezer. She had just put the bread and the peanut butter on the table and was trying to remember where she put the new jar of strawberry jelly when the phone rang.

It was Helen, just as she expected. Her daughter didn't even ask where she was this time. "Mom, do you remember me talking about the Cartwrights? They live near us. We went to that dinner they had with all those politicians and Princess Diana's brother was there?"

"I remember. You said it was ritzy and you had a really good time."

"Very posh. Everything just so. That really was a lovely evening. Anyhow... I see Louise Cartwright now and then, and Malcolm and Arthur golf together. So we're friends, not close friends, but we are friends."

Mrs. B didn't say anything.

"Mom, are you still there?"

"Of course I'm still here. I'm waiting for you to say why you're telling me all this."

"Oh. Arthur Cartwright was arrested. Securities fraud."

Mrs. B said, "Do you have money invested with him?"

"No," Helen said. "We've had the same financial advisor for years, but he's getting older and we had talked about having Arthur manage our investments. Malcolm just mentioned it again last week."

"Was his wife involved in the business?" Mrs. B asked.

"No, I'm sure she wasn't. Louise managed their social life."

"How's she handling all this?"

"That's why I called," Helen said. "I haven't talked to Louise, and I don't know whether I should call her or not. It just happened yesterday. What do you think, Mom? Should I call her?"

"Not so soon, no," Mrs. B said. "Let me ask you, do you like her, or do you just feel obliged?"

"I do like her," Helen said. "I feel bad for her. She must be mortified. And who knows what her financial situation will be now."

"Well, then, drop her a kind note. Just say you're thinking about her, and nothing more. That way the door's open. She'll come to you if she wants to."

"Thanks, Mom." Mrs. B could hear a faint whistle in the background while her daughter spoke. "I didn't know what to do," Helen said. "I remember how you told me that whenever Leo got arrested, Mrs. Komar would stop over the next morning with a cake or a pie and you knew all she wanted was information. I don't want to be like that. Hold on a minute." When Helen got back to the phone she said, "I had to shut off the teakettle. So, where did you go this morning?"

Mrs. B thought for a moment. She didn't want to lie, but she didn't want to tell the whole truth, either. It never did any good to tell Helen too much of her business. "Anne came over this morning and picked me up, and the two of us went to a friend's house, somebody from the Senior Center. She lives on Eleanor Street."

"Well, that's nice. Did you get that brochure I ordered for you? For the retirement village? You know, Mom, there are some really lovely places right outside the city where you could live. I asked them to send you some information..."

"I got it."

"Well, what did you think?'

"I didn't think anything. I didn't look at them."

"Well, you should take a look, Mom. I did a virtual tour of some of these places on the internet, and they're very nice."

"I'm sure they are."

"You'd really like them, Mom. They..."

Enough was suddenly enough. "Helen, I'm not moving."

It was as if her daughter didn't even hear her. "Mom, this place is so pretty. They have a little pond with picnic tables around it. And they all have these big rooms you can watch television in, so you don't have to watch TV by yourself all the time."

Mrs. B said, "I like to watch TV by myself. I don't know why you keep talking about this. You were just here at Easter. Everything was fine. All of a sudden you want me to move."

Helen's voice took a turn. "Mom, I bet you have your front door open right now, don't you? You really need to be careful. Everything wasn't fine when I was there. That guy got beat up right around the corner at the pizza shop. And then you fainted and Jimmy had to write me to tell me about it. I don't think you should be in that house all by yourself."

"Oh, for goodness sake, Helen. Robbie Denton's brother-in-law beat him up. I doubt Robbie's brother-in-law is lurking around, waiting to punch me in the nose."

"Mom, don't make jokes."

"I'm not joking, I'm stating a fact."

"Mom, seriously. There are drug addicts in Burchfield."

They both must have thought about Leo then, because neither of them said anything for a while. Finally, Mrs. B said, softly, "Honey, I'm sure there are drug addicts in your neighborhood, too. They're just more secretive about it. You know how Burchfield is. Everybody knows everything about everybody."

Helen paused before she spoke. "Mama, I worry about Leo every goddamn day. I can't worry about you, too. It's too much."

Mrs. B said, "There's no need to swear."

Helen's voice softened. "Malcolm and I would help pay your rent in the new place. We already talked about it." She paused, then said, "Mama, I'm so far away. If anything ever happened…"

"If something happens, I'll call Jimmy."

"Jimmy!" Helen said. "What's he going to do? Beat the robber to death with his broom?"

Mrs. B took a breath. This was important, and she had to use the right words. Quietly, she said, "Honey, I know you think you know what's best for me, I know you mean well. But you want me to move because you worry, and that's not fair. I'm perfectly fine right where I am. I'm a block from the church, a block from the Senior Center. You might think Jimmy's not much help but he shovels my snow in the winter and he takes me grocery shopping. He's really a very good neighbor."

Helen's voice took on a pleading tone. "I know that, Mom. I know that. Jimmy's always been a good neighbor. I just want you to be somewhere where there's, I don't know, supervision. Mama, if you don't like Countryside Village, I could find a Catholic place where they'd have bingo, and…"

Mrs. B didn't want to upset her daughter, she really didn't, but it appeared she had no choice. "Helen, Helen, you're not listening to me. Listen to me." Her voice was firm now. "I don't want to play bingo with a bunch of strangers. I want to go to St. Mary's Senior Center, where all my friends are. And when I come home I want to watch TV, by myself, in my own house. You might be ashamed of the house you grew up in, but your father and I worked hard to buy this house. I'm not going anywhere, and you just have to get used to that fact."

Helen said, "Mom, I can't talk to you anymore," and hung up.

Mrs. B placed the phone back in the receiver slowly. Her heart ached. But she had to do it, didn't she? She had to say what she'd said to Helen. She didn't have any choice.

And it was done now. It was done, and there was no sense dwelling on it.

She went to the kitchen and rummaged around in the cupboard until she found the jar of strawberry jelly hiding behind a can of peaches. She mixed the lemonade in a tan plastic pitcher with a white lid. The pitcher was way too big but she couldn't find her little one. She stirred it with her long wooden spoon, then sat down at the kitchen table with a sandwich at her left and a folded newspaper to her right. With her #2 pencil in hand, she wrote in the answer to 6 down and then 8 across.

31

Mrs. B sat on her porch most of that afternoon with a cool glass of lemonade, finishing one book and starting another. Jimmy came out to wash down his porch furniture, and the two of them talked for a while. Mr. Bacigal waved to her from his front yard. Michelle, Kelly's mom, got home from work and stopped by to say hello. Altogether, it was a pleasant afternoon and she didn't get out of her white rocker until it was almost suppertime.

She took a TV dinner to the living room and turned the television to the classic movie channel, which was halfway through *State Fair*. Mrs. B left it on, but picked up her crossword puzzle. She wasn't a fan of the movie. She loved Dick Haymes, but she never really believed that Dana Andrews was in love with Jeanne Crain. He was too much of a smooth talker.

She finished the Chicago puzzle and started the one in last week's Guardian. She hadn't finished a single one of these Guardian puzzles yet, but she kept trying. Every time there was a Dick Haymes song, her attention went back to *State Fair*, and she soon drifted to her own memories of long-ago school picnics at Kennywood. Her mother and uncle playing cards with the neighbors. Tables of picnic baskets full of bread and cheese and kielbasa. Eating cucumbers and onions floating in sugar and vinegar water from a jar wrapped in a white towel, Uncle fishing them out and putting them in her bare hands with a long wooden spoon. Walking around the amusement park with her girlfriends, how excited they were to show off their picnic outfits, how happy they were every time they ran into another classmate. Listening to the band and watching the older girls dance, their skirts softly moving to the music. Candy apples that got your whole face sticky. That hot summer day she was waiting in line with Norma Bartel to ride The Whip, and Stush Majeski was in line behind them and he was telling a story to his friends and he threw his arms out and knocked both their sun hats off. He was so apologetic that she and Norma decided they were sweet on him. All the rest of the summer they would beg their mothers to send them to the butcher shop so he could wait on them.

Mrs. B didn't even notice the movie again until it was over, when she put down the puzzle and went into the kitchen. She got back to her chair with a bowl of fruit cocktail just as *The Enchanted Cottage* was starting. Though she'd seen it many times before, she let herself fall under the spell of the story. She watched all the way through to the end without moving and even sat for a moment afterward, remembering the tender kiss in the doorway in the last scene. Then she went to the junk drawer in the kitchen and came back to her rocker with a pad of paper. She turned down the sound, picked up her pencil, and wrote:

What I know about Alice:

She has cousins in Chicago. (hearsay)

She has two daughters. (known)

Her daughters don't speak to her. (known)

She spoiled her daughters. (hearsay, but from more than one source)

She has a workshop and subscribes to magazines and has books about building things and fixing things. (known)

She can build and fix things. (hearsay, more than one source)

She likes to garden. She subscribes to magazines about gardening. (known)

She really does have a beautiful garden, Mrs. B thought. Mostly perennials, so it's probably something she's given a lot of thought to over the years. She wondered why Alice didn't grow vegetables. Albert used to grow onions and tomatoes, but of course their little house had a bigger yard and he cut down that tree in the backyard so the vegetable patch got sun all day. Maybe Alice's garden doesn't get enough sun. Maybe she just prefers growing flowers.

What else?

She may be illegitimate. (hearsay)

Her father may have been someone very rich. (hearsay, more than one source)

But of course, that was the kind of rumor that spread easily, even if it wasn't true. She didn't know if she could give a lot of credence to that.

What else?

She owns an emerald necklace that belonged to her mother. (hearsay, more than one source)

Mrs. B was pretty sure that necklace existed. Patty said she saw it. Alice knew her neighbor well enough to give her a spare key to her house, and there really didn't seem to be any reason for Patty to lie.

Her daughter's boyfriend tried to break into Alice's house. (hearsay, more than one source)

He may have been looking for the necklace. There may have been an innocent explanation, but Mrs. B couldn't think of what that would be. Of course, maybe it wasn't related to Alice at all. Maybe Jane's boyfriend was a burglar and broke into houses all the time. Though he did get caught, which made her reconsider whether he had much experience at being a burglar. The fact that he ran from Patty made it seem unlikely he was dangerous. So maybe he wanted that necklace really badly. Or maybe Jane browbeat him into looking for it.

It was sad that Alice gave her neighbor a key to her house, but didn't give Jane one. Did she change the locks after her girls moved out? Alice mustn't trust Jane. She might not trust either of her daughters.

That must be awful, being estranged from your daughter.

Mrs. B looked at the clock. It was nearly 10:30, and she was starting to feel sleepy. It had been a long day. She turned the page and wrote another title.

What I don't know:

Where the emerald necklace is.

Where Alice is.

Mrs. B looked at the page for quite a while before she put her pencil down. Then she shut and locked the front door, washed the dishes and put on her pajamas.

32

Mrs. B set her book on the nightstand and shut off the light. She closed her eyes, but before long she opened them again.

It didn't happen often, but when it did, this was when it happened. The worrying. During the day, Mrs. B was disciplined. She concentrated on the task at hand. She'd learned to keep her worries at bay and they had to wait until now, until nighttime, if they were going to creep up on her.

She shut her eyes again and started to count her blessings. A comfortable bed. A nice pillow. Food to eat today, and lemonade to drink. She'd had the good fortune to have spent many years married to a man she loved. She had two children she loved.

Alice's children didn't care about her. Her little granddaughter did care, though. Cassie cared. The girl's round, pale-green eyes pleaded with Mrs. B. *I love my grandma. Is my grandma all right?*

Mrs. B looked at her bedroom ceiling. Is this anxious feeling really about Alice? Maybe it isn't that at all. Maybe I'm worried about that phone call with Helen.

Mrs. B knew she was lucky to have a daughter who loved her so much that it became a problem, but this was one problem she didn't know how to solve. She was happy here, in her own bed, in her own home. She didn't want to leave, but if she stayed here, could she lose her daughter?

Had she done the right thing tonight, standing up to Helen? What if her daughter decided she couldn't take all the worrying anymore? What if Helen felt she had to detach herself, to disappear from her mother's life? Helen couldn't come to visit all the time, and that was understandable. She lived on the other side of an ocean. But what if Helen decided she would only do her duty, send a card for birthdays, flowers for Mother's Day? What if Mrs. B never saw her daughter again?

Helen's calls and letters meant everything to Mrs. B. She planned for weeks when she came to visit, buying groceries to make Helen's favorite foods, turning down plans with her friends to spend time, precious time, with her little girl.

She didn't want to lose her daughter. She couldn't. It was unthinkable.

And it was unlikely. Extremely unlikely. She was being ridiculous. Helen had always been attentive, and they'd had fights before. They'd get through this.

Alice's daughters weren't looking for Alice. What if Alice went down that path behind the restaurant, or maybe some other deserted road? They'd seen lots of wooded areas in Hopewell. What if she'd fallen and had been lying there all week, with nothing to eat or drink? What if Alice had called out, and no one had heard her?

She was going to give herself nightmares. Lying in bed worrying wasn't going to help Alice one bit. If that's what happened, there was nothing Mrs. B could do about it from miles away, in the middle of the night.

Maybe none of this was what was really bothering her, though. Maybe this anxious feeling was about what it was usually about. Maybe it was about Leo.

Mrs. B didn't know where her son was, and she hadn't known for so long now. Is that why she'd fixated on trying to find a missing woman, a woman she barely knew?

How long had Leo had been gone now? More than ten years, easily. Could it be twenty? Mrs. B was always so good with numbers but she sometimes had a mental block when it came to Leo's disappearance.

On rare occasions, a postcard would arrive from California. There'd be no message, but in her address she'd recognize Leo's shaky handwriting. Every time, she thought about keeping the card but ended up throwing it away. It hurt too much to look at it. Every time, she'd say a novena for Leo. She tried to remember when the last postcard was. She couldn't remember.

She looked at the clock, then shut her eyes again. Lying in bed in the dark, with one fearful notion after another. Who did that help? Nobody.

Mrs. B began to say a rosary. She didn't need the beads, she'd done this a million times. In the name of the Father, and of the Son, and of the Holy Ghost... The familiar ritual lulled her thoughts, and she was asleep before she'd finished the third decade. But during the night she tossed and she turned. One dream after another, forgotten as soon as they were over.

She awoke in a still silence. She knew without looking at the clock that it was the middle of the night, but she turned over and checked the time anyhow. 3:15. She took a deep breath and said a prayer.

The world seems so different when you wake up in the middle of the night. She did feel calmer now, not as restless as before. Maybe she'd dreamt something nice, though she couldn't remember what that might be.

And then she thought: Over the hill.

Well, that doesn't make any sense. Where did that come from? It seems important, though. Did she dream she was over a hill?

Was she worried about being past her prime? What did that have to do with anything? She'd been past her prime for a long time, and so were most of her friends. That didn't mean their lives were over. There was plenty of fun left to be had. She could still do a crossword puzzle, read a book, take care of her house in her own imperfect way. Despite what Helen seemed to think.

But now Mrs. B was awake again. Well, if she was up, she might as well be productive. She slid her feet into her bedroom slippers, went to the living room, got the list she had written and brought it back to bed.

What I know about Alice. She read it twice, then went back in her mind to last Sunday, trying to replay every step from the church parking lot to Supper Club, from dessert to their wait for Alice. Then every step of their search for her. Where they went, what was said. There had to be something she'd missed.

She walked through it once, and then walked through it again. More slowly the second time, so she could look for details. The ride to Barnum's. Waiting in the car in the restaurant parking lot. Their search through the restaurant. The store with the popsicles. The conversations with Jane and Tree, with Patty, with Carmella. Her conversations with Anne. Their trip to the police station. And then, back through the whole thing again, through it and around it and up and down until suddenly things snapped together and… there it was.

It was possible. Not certain, but certainly possible. It made sense. It made perfect sense, when she thought about it. She couldn't totally put everything together, but there had to be some sort of connection because everything about it made sense.

I'll call Anne in the morning, before we go to Mass, and ask her to bring that picture of Alice, Mrs. B decided. She glanced at the clock again. A little after 4:00. She fluffed her pillow and rolled over, pulled the light blanket over her shoulders.

The pragmatist in Mrs. B told her that this could very well be one of those things that seems so clear in the middle of the night but doesn't stand up to the light of day. But only a few minutes went by before she was fast asleep, and she slept soundly until morning.

Sunday

33

What a beautiful day it was. The air was cool and fresh on her way to morning Mass, and there wasn't a cloud in the sky. It really was a perfect day for a Sunday drive.

Mrs. B crossed the brick sidewalk in front of the church, climbed its three wide steps and entered through the open double doors. She dipped the tips of her fingers in the holy water font. The white marble felt cool to her touch. She blessed herself as she walked down the aisle. Genuflecting, she sat in the pew where she always sat, where she'd been sitting since she and Albert moved to Burchfield all those years ago.

She looked around. Church wasn't crowded this morning. It seldom was anymore, except for holidays. People seemed to want to go to Mass on Saturday night, especially in the summertime.

She kicked the kneeler down to use as a footstool. No one else was in her pew. In the other direction, across the center aisle, sat a little girl in red shorts and a frilly pink top. She'll be starting kindergarten in the fall, Mrs. B thought. A young woman sat next to the little girl. She held a baby dressed in a Pirates sleeper and a tiny baseball cap, which he fussed with until she finally took it off. The young mother rocked the baby back and forth gently when they stood for the first hymn. When the little girl looked across the aisle, Mrs. B smiled and waved. The little girl waved back shyly, then quickly turned toward her mom.

Mrs. B could see the back of Anne's head on the other side of the church. Anne was in her regular pew, which was closer to the front and across the center aisle.

Mrs. B liked to go to 9:30 Mass because it was Father Clancy, and she liked Father Clancy. He didn't always make the wisest choices, but he was a good man deep inside, and that was what mattered. Father always had something nice to say at the homily. Today was no exception.

"I was fishing yesterday up at Pymatuning. Didn't catch anything worth eating, had to stop at the supermarket on the way home to buy fish sticks for supper." That got a little chuckle from the parishioners. "While I was out there fishing, I got to thinking about St. Peter. Jesus saying, 'Come on, Peter'"—Father held his arms out, beckoning—"'Come on, walk over to me. Walk on the water.' We always talk about the part of the story where Peter gets scared. He loses his faith and he sinks. But we never talk about the faith Peter had to have to walk out on that water in the first place, and that's what I was thinking about yesterday when I was fishing. Even if Peter had it for a minute—think about it, that kind of faith. To walk out there on water, even for a second, and trust that you'd be held up by faith. Could you do that? That's what I asked myself, too. Could I do that? And you got to figure, I'm a priest! I should be able to!" That got a bigger chuckle.

It turned into a very nice homily and, as expected, a short one. Father Clancy always aimed for a short sermon when it was a pretty day outside. Mass went quickly, and before she knew it Mrs. B was walking down the church steps with Anne. The two ladies headed toward the parking lot.

"I'm glad I remembered you were bringing the convertible," Mrs. B said. She lowered herself into the passenger seat of Anne's grandson's shiny blue Mustang and pulled a flowered babushka out of her pocket. The blue daisies on the scarf were almost the same shade as the car's dashboard. She tied the babushka under her chin, peering into the side mirror to comb her white bangs down with her fingers.

"Now wouldn't it be a sin to leave this beautiful car in my garage on a day like this?" Anne waved her arm toward the sky as she opened the door on the driver's side. "It was practically begging me to drive it." She bent over to put her purse on the floor and reached for a framed photo in the back seat. She held the picture of Alice and her granddaughter up for Mrs. B to see, then tossed it onto the seat again.

"Good," Mrs. B said. "Someone needs to be looking for Alice, and apparently we've been elected. So we're stopping in Hopewell?"

"Yes." Anne buckled her seat belt with an emphatic *click*. Mrs. B sat back in her seat. Anne turned the radio volume louder than it needed to be, and Benny Goodman's band blasted through the

speakers. As they drove past the bar, the men loaf-
ing out front turned toward the music with puzzled
faces. Anne glanced at Mrs. B, chin held high, and
the two of them giggled halfway up the avenue.

34

The sun was hot but it wasn't yet that searing-summer-afternoon sort of hot. Mrs. B tied a second knot in her babushka when they got onto the main road. A big sixteen-wheeler lent temporary shade as it roared by, and then Anne settled into a comfortable spot in the right lane. Strip malls gave way to country hillsides, towns with ranch houses, vegetable gardens, lavender and tiger lilies. Frank Sinatra's voice boomed through the speakers, *Love and Marriage* making its way to Mrs. B's ears over the traffic noise. She had never been a Sinatra fan; she'd always much preferred Bing Crosby. But when Anne began to sing along, Mrs. B joined in.

By the time they got to Barnum's, the parking lot was more than halfway full. Anne parked next to the tiger, in the shade of the giant lion tamer. Mrs. B got out of the car and walked toward the back of the building without saying a word to Anne.

Anne picked up the photo of Alice and followed her. "Ed! Where are you going?"

Mrs. B turned, preoccupied. "Sorry. Around back."

The back door of the restaurant was propped open, just like it was last Sunday. Mrs. B stopped at the berry bushes and picked a few, staring down the path alongside. Anne tucked the photo frame under her arm and picked a handful too. The surrounding trees swayed in a gentle breeze, making sunshine and shadow patterns everywhere. The two of them stood there for a while, eating berries and staring into the woods. Neither of them spoke.

Finally Anne said, "Let's go in and see if anyone's seen Alice." They walked through the open back door and into the ladies room to wash the sticky berry juice from their hands. Then they went to the little podium at the front entrance.

The restaurant was bustling but there were still open tables in view. A little blonde girl with her hair in a long ponytail picked up two menus as they approached, smiling her best professional smile. "Two?"

Anne said, "We're looking for our friend." She started to hold out the picture, but the blonde girl waved her arm around the room as she looked toward the front door, where more people were coming in. "You're welcome to look for her if you like." The ponytail swished as she turned toward a grey-haired gent and three women. She picked up two more menus and gave them her smile. "Four for lunch?"

Mrs. B turned to Anne. "Let's try that little store first."

Anne tossed Alice's picture onto the back seat again. They pulled up in front of the store behind two motorcycles and, just as Mrs. B was taking off her babushka, Tiny and Boom walked down the steps from the store. They each lit a cigarette. It was like deja vu.

"Look who it is, Tiny," Boom said, putting his lighter in a shirt pocket. "The Mustang ladies."

Tiny nodded in their direction.

"Out for a Sunday drive?" Boom asked.

"We're looking for a friend of ours," Mrs. B said. "Maybe you've seen her."

Boom was walking around the car, touching the fenders with his fingertips. "Maybe." He bent down and looked at the chrome. "Little dent in the chrome here. Can't hardly see it, though. Probably no one would notice unless they were looking for it."

"I've been really careful with this car," Anne said. "If there's a dent, it was my grandson's doing."

"Nobody's gonna notice it unless they're looking for it," Boom said as he walked around to the driver's side. He looked in the back seat, then reached over and picked up the photograph. "This Alice's granddaughter?"

Anne looked at Mrs. B. "You know Alice?" Mrs. B asked. Despite herself, her heart started to pound.

"Just met her this week," Boom said, still looking at the picture. "Down the professor's." He set the framed photo back on the seat and turned to Mrs. B. "She one of them mail-order brides? That's what me and Tiny thought, but we didn't want to ask. Didn't seem polite somehow."

Mrs. B took a deep breath as Boom talked. Her heart was still beating fast, but when she spoke, her voice was steady. "I'm not sure how they met, to tell you the truth."

"Bakes a good pie," Tiny said.

"Yeah, she fed us cherry pie this morning. Those sour cherries from up over the hill by the church," Boom said. "That where you ladies headed, over the professor's?"

Mrs. B turned to Anne. Anne's face was white and her blue eyes were round as saucers. They nodded slowly, both of them trying their best to look nonchalant.

"We been down there the last couple days, me and Tiny," Boom said. "The professor asked us to be on the lookout for 55-gallon drums, and we got him some Thursday, took them down Friday morning. He's building a windmill. Me and Tiny, we been helping out. Alice too." He shook his head admiringly. "Don't find that every day, a woman can bake and still tell a wrench from a pair of pliers."

"There's pie left," Tiny said, dipping his head to address Mrs. B. "We didn't eat it all, though I was sorely tempted." He rubbed his stomach contentedly.

I knew it, Mrs. B thought. I knew it. It all makes sense. She asked, "Could you tell us, what's the best way to get to the professor's house from here?"

Boom looked the ladies over, right down to their church shoes. "Path behind Barnum's the closest, but you don't want to take that, not in your nice Sunday clothes. You want to drive down over the hill, but it's tricky. Like a switchback." He pulled a little spiral-topped notebook from his back pocket, then searched through his jeans and pulled out a stubby pencil. He called Anne over, and she watched as he drew. "Now when you get there, you want to park here, you don't want to take the Mustang up that dirt road. You'll have to walk a little bit, but it's not far. There's a row of apple trees here and right beyond that you'll see the house…"

Over the hill. That's where we'll find Alice. Over the hill.

35

Neither of them said anything until the blue Mustang got to the bottom of the long road at the end of the hill. An abandoned gas station sat lonely and alone, backed by a steep bank overgrown with sumac trees. Anne pulled in and turned down the radio, then turned off the engine.

The two women sat in silence for a full minute. Then Anne said, "What the hell?"

Mrs. B shook her head. She needed a moment to think.

The little gas station was boarded up, and Xs were written across the plywood with black spray paint.

The gas pumps were still there. They were the old, rounded kind, red and white, and rusted around the edges. One entrance to the lot, the one where they came in, was still in good repair. Chunks of crumbled concrete were stacked at the other side. Anne's going to have to turn around, Mrs. B thought, and go out the way we came in.

"Thank goodness Alice is all right," Mrs. B said finally.

"We've been imagining all sorts of horrible things," Anne said, "and all the time the woman's out here baking cherry pies."

They were quiet again. A sparrow flew by and sat at the top of the gas pump. Another joined it.

"With a professor," Anne said. "Now what's that all about?"

Mrs. B said, "I think it's the professor they talked about at the little store where we got the popsicles."

Anne turned toward her. "What?"

"Remember, the woman at the store asked those motorcycle boys if they were going over the hill. She wanted them to tell a professor something because he didn't have a phone," Mrs. B said. "Solar batteries. She had just gotten in some solar batteries."

"Jesus, Mary and Joseph, how could you remember that?" Anne said.

"I usually remember things when I pay attention," Mrs. B said.

A grackle flew toward the sparrows and they took off for the old garage roof.

Anne spoke up. "Well, we ought to go over there, don't you think? Make sure she's okay?"

"Oh, yes, definitely. We do need to make sure she's okay."

"You know, maybe this professor kidnapped her," Anne said.

"And forced her to bake cherry pies?" Mrs. B said.

Anne started to laugh. "No, that wouldn't make sense. Gee, I'm so glad she's alright."

"Me, too," Mrs. B said. "Me, too."

Silence again. Wild daisies were growing in a crack in the concrete near the ruined exit. They bent gently when a breeze went by.

"Do you think Alice is a mail-order bride?" Anne asked.

"I doubt it. It would be awfully coincidental that her mail-order man lived right near the restaurant we went to for Supper Club," Mrs. B said. "Listen, when we get there, let's not say anything about looking for her all week. We don't want her to feel guilty about us worrying, and there's no reason for her to feel that way. She doesn't know yet that she has good friends like us."

"Well, what do we say to her, then?" Anne cocked her head and made a face. "We were just in the neighborhood?"

"Oh, I don't know. We'll think of something. Maybe she won't ask."

Anne tapped her pale pink fingernails on the steering wheel. She made a tsk sound, shook her head and turned on the car. "Oh, all right. But she better tell us why she's out here. The suspense is killing me."

36

The dirt road was mostly red clay, so it wasn't too dusty. The row of apple trees was on their right, just like Boom said it would be. Anne and Mrs. B were halfway up the drive when they saw a long clothesline hung between a cabin's rough porch pillar and the low, thick branch of a large ancient sycamore. White sheets and colorful towels fluttered in the breeze, held up high by long, thin poles staggered between them. A dog barked somewhere close by, and then they heard a woman's voice. "Sparky? What did you see, Sparky? Did you see a bunny rabbit?"

Mrs. B turned to Anne. "Is that her? I think that's her." She began to walk just a little bit faster.

Anne kept up easily with a long-legged stride. "When's the last time you saw a clothes prop?" Anne said.

A yellow retriever came toward them carrying a worn tennis ball. The ladies turned the final bend in the road and there was Alice, plain as the nose on your face, taking washing down from the line.

Mrs. B and Anne caught her eye and waved.

Alice turned from the laundry, clothespins in her hand, her astonishment tempered with a big smile. She waved back. "What a nice surprise!" she said as she threw the clothespins in a wicker basket on the ground. "Oh, I'm glad I made those cherry pies this morning."

Both Anne and Mrs. B worked hard to make sure their faces didn't betray the only question on their minds: *What in God's good name was going on here?*

Alice reached up to grab the end of a sheet and instinctively Mrs. B and Anne both hurried over to help. Anne and Alice folded the sheet while Mrs. B approached the red towel next to it. It wasn't easy for her to reach. She tugged the corner to pull it down, took the clothespins off and tossed them into the basket.

She couldn't reach the washcloth next to it, and didn't want to move the clothes prop for fear of dirtying the rest of the laundry. She headed toward another towel farther down the line just as Sparky wandered over, mouth full of tennis ball, tail high in the air. She bent to pet him, then took the sloppy ball from his mouth and tossed it.

Mrs. B looked down at her wet hands and decided she'd better leave the rest of the wash to Alice and Anne. Sparky pranced back and Mrs. B tossed the ball again.

"Oh, this is so nice!" Alice was saying to Anne. "I didn't know we were going to have company!"

Alice's back was to Mrs. B as Anne helped her fold a blanket. Anne shot a meaningful look over Alice's shoulder, and Mrs. B nodded. Not saying anything was harder than she thought. "How old is Sparky?" Mrs. B asked as she bent down toward the dog, then tossed the ball again.

"I don't know," Alice said, dropping a couple of clothespins into the basket. "Young, he seems to me. Three, four, would that be your guess? He's got a lot of energy." She looked toward the sun. "Close to lunchtime, I bet," she said. "Let me finish this up and I'll make sandwiches. I baked bread yesterday, and there's some cucumbers in the garden. Oh, it's so nice to have ladies here! All I've seen is men all week." She looked at the clothes she was wearing, then waved a hand self-consciously down the front of her. "Oh, my gosh, look how I'm dressed! You'll have to excuse my outfit. I had to borrow these."

Truth was, Alice looked adorable. She wore denim overalls, too big for her and rolled at the ankle, with a man's white t-shirt. Her hair was tied up in a red polka-dot scarf. And her face—well, it glowed. Pink cheeks, bright eyes and a smile that showed a fading but still visible set of dimples.

Alice carried the basket of laundry to a bench in a large boot room by the back door, next to an old-fashioned wringer washer and a sink. Anne followed her into the cabin, but Mrs. B stood in the doorway for a second, taking everything in.

The boot room was sunny through the open door, but beyond it the entrance to the kitchen was darker and noticeably cooler. A stove stood to her left and beyond it a counter with a window above it. Sunlight shone through the open window, which meant no trees above it, which probably meant a kitchen garden below, Mrs. B surmised. To her right were a series of shelves, two tall rows with a lower row between. On the tall rows sat store-bought cans of corn and peas along with Mason jars full of tomatoes and peaches. More, bigger jars surrounded them, filled to various heights with macaroni, rice, navy beans, kidney beans, split peas, lentils. The low row held pots and pans, and its top shelf, covered with dish towels, held three pies, one half eaten and covered by a large glass bowl inverted over it. In the center of the room was a square wooden table, old but serviceable. It was clean and bare. Four well-worn wooden chairs surrounded it.

Alice was at the stove, waving them in. "Please, sit down. I'll put on water for tea. There's a peppermint bush on the side of the cabin." Anne sat at the table while Alice poured water into a white enamel pot. She set it on the stove to boil, then went to the boot room. Mrs. B stepped out of her way and Alice reached under the sink, emerging with a pair of pruning shears. "You two just make yourselves at home. Oh, I'm so glad you came!" Alice said as she headed back outside.

Mrs. B washed her hands at the sink and dried them on a white dishtowel with thin green stripes. She sat down next to Anne at the table. Anne whispered as she raised an eyebrow, "Don't we feel silly. She's happy as a clam."

It was true. Alice really did look happy, much happier than she had last week when they drove to Supper Club.

"We didn't have any way of knowing," Mrs. B said quietly. "We're her friends, don't forget. It's our job to care about her."

"That's true," Anne said. "You know, my grandmother used to make peppermint tea. I haven't had a hot cup of peppermint tea in ages."

37

Mrs. B and Anne watched Alice's head bob by the kitchen window. As soon as their friend was out of sight, Anne leaned toward Mrs. B and said, "I'm about to die of curiosity! What do you think is going on here?"

"I don't know," Mrs. B said. "It doesn't look proper, but it doesn't feel improper. Does that make sense?"

Anne tilted her head and grinned. "All I know is, she looks twenty years younger than she did last Sunday."

The scent of peppermint filled the room when Alice returned with green, leafy sprigs. She set them on the counter next to three large cucumbers, then began to collect the leaves into a little bowl. A *thump* made Anne and Mrs. B both turn their heads toward the boot room.

"Don't mind me, ladies." A balding, white-haired gent with big brown eyes slapped a pair of worn work gloves onto the bench next to the laundry basket. He turned his back to them to wash at the sink with a bar of Fels-Naptha soap. A white ponytail hung over his collar. As he dried his hands on a worn terrycloth towel, he said, "Just came in to get my lunch. I can eat outside while you ladies talk."

Alice said, "No, no, no, you stay, Harvey. I'm making cucumber sandwiches and tea. Oh, that's girly, isn't it? I can make you a cheese sandwich."

Harvey walked toward the table. "I'll eat anything you put in front of me."

Alice said, "Harvey, these are the ladies who drove me to Barnum's last Sunday. They're from Burchfield, from the Senior Center."

"Ed," Mrs. B said, nodding toward him. "And this is Anne."

Harvey shook both their hands with a meaty paw. "Well, I'm in your debt now, aren't I? Brought me the best farm hand I've ever had."

"I bet I am," Alice said, laughing.

"You bet you are," Harvey said, sitting at the table just as Mrs. B and Anne got up to help Alice with lunch.

"No, no, this won't take any time at all," Alice said as she bustled over to the sink, returning with a paring knife. She began to peel a cucumber. "You all just sit and talk."

There had to be a simple explanation for all this. Mrs. B asked Harvey, "Did you teach at one of the local colleges?"

"Me?" Harvey said. "Oh, no, no, I was an engineer at Westinghouse."

"Oh," Mrs. B said, embarrassed. "I thought…"

"I know, I know, the nickname," Harvey said, waving her misconception away with his hand. "Folks out here started calling me professor because I invent things. Like the professor on *Gilligan's Island.*" He got up from his chair to pull a loaf of dark bread from an old-fashioned wooden breadbox near the boot room. He brought it to the table. "You have to be inventive when you live like I do. Comes with the territory."

He turned his back to them as he rooted through a drawer. Alice was busy with the tea. Anne tilted her head down and looked up over her nose at Mrs. B with big, wide eyes, rolling her right hand in circles as if to say, 'Hurry up already!' Mrs. B shook her head, but Anne said to Harvey, "So, how long have you two known each other?"

Before he could reply, Alice said, "Harvey, will you run out to the spring house and get me that nice cream cheese we got yesterday? And bring me some dill on your way back?"

38

The water on the stove was boiling. Alice dumped the bowl of mint leaves in, then shut it off and sat at the table with Anne and Mrs. B. "I didn't even think how awful this must look," she said, shaking her head back and forth as she spoke. "Honestly, Harvey's been a real gentleman. He's teaching me all kinds of things about self-sufficient farming."

Mrs. B said, "How did you two meet? Was it behind Barnum's, at the berry bush?"

"Yes!" Alice said. "How did you know?"

Anne turned to Mrs. B, eyebrows raised as if to ask the same question. Mrs. B pretended she didn't see Anne. Alice said, "At Barnum's, when I left the ladies room, the back door to the restaurant was open and I saw the berry bushes. I went out to take a look, see what kind they were. There's a path right there, and Harvey came walking up with a bucket in his hand.

"He said hello, and I said hello, and the two of us got to talking. He told me he had a farm and he was attempting to live off the grid, create all his own energy. I'd read about that sort of thing in magazines. I helped him pick berries for a while, and he told me about the greenhouse he made out of old windows, the windmill he was getting ready to build. It was all so interesting! I asked him question after question and at one point I said I wished I could see all the things he was talking about. Harvey said, 'No time like the present,' turned his back to me and started walking down the path. I followed him without even thinking about it."

Alice walked around the table to where Harvey had been sitting. She cut slices of bread, talking all the while. "Now that you're here and I see how it must look, you must think I'm so foolish, following a man I didn't even know. But at the time, honestly, I didn't think a thing of it. I just wanted to see the farm, see the rainwater irrigation system in the garden, see the blender that runs on solar power. It never crossed my mind that I shouldn't. Down the path I went, right behind him.

"Harvey showed me all around, and I had a million questions. I completely lost track of time and before I knew it, it was late and I knew you would have all gone home. I asked Harvey if he could drive me to Burchfield. He's got a big red truck out back. It looks beat up but it runs good. A little noisy, that's all. Anyhow he said sure, he'd run me home. I left my purse in your car, Anne, it's probably still in your trunk. But Patty next door has a key to my house, so I knew I could get in.

"Anyhow, just when we were getting ready to head out the door, Harvey started talking about this windmill he's building. He had the blueprints all drawn up and I asked could I see them and the next thing I knew it was dark and Harvey has trouble driving on the highway when it's dark. His eyes, you know how it is at our age. So he said why don't I stay the night, I could take his bed and he'd sleep on the cot in the back room. And really, I didn't have any reason to go home, not with Maizie gone. Maizie's my dog. She passed away a few weeks ago. My house is so empty without little Maizie. So I figured one night wouldn't do any harm, and now here it is

Monday, I've been here more than a week. I don't know where the time's gone."

Mrs. B shook her head gently. "Today's Sunday."

"Sunday!" Alice said, walking over to the counter with the bread as Harvey came in, filling the air with the scent of dill. "Why was I doing laundry on Sunday? Harvey, why didn't you tell me today was Sunday?"

Harvey set a bowl of cream cheese on the counter, then put the dill on a cutting board. "I don't know, you didn't ask me. You want this chopped?"

"Please." The two worked side by side, covering bread with cream cheese, then dill, then cucumber slices, then cutting the sandwiches into quarters. Mrs. B and Anne watched them for a while. Then Anne winked at Mrs. B, and Mrs. B smiled and settled back in her chair.

39

"Nice meeting you ladies." Harvey nodded as he headed toward the back door, work gloves in hand. Alice was slicing crumbly-crusted hunks of cherry pie.

"Just a little one for me," Anne said.

"Me, too," Mrs. B said. "Don't know how much room I have after those delicious sandwiches."

Alice turned the stove on. "I had pie this morning, but I'll have another cup of tea while you eat."

Mrs. B took a bite, turned to Anne and said, "Those boys were right."

Anne nodded. "Alice, this is excellent pie."

Alice beamed. "Thanks. Kind of my specialty, pie crust."

"Do you do something particular to make it so tender?"

"Measure out the butter, measure out the flour, mix them together then fold in the water," she recited in a sing-song voice. "Mrs. Butler, my chemistry teacher, taught me that. Peach pies, we made. She took me under her wing, Mrs. Butler, me being the only girl in chemistry. Physics, too, senior year. All the other girls took secretarial, or homemaking. But if you think about it, baking really is chemistry, isn't it?"

Mrs. B nodded while Anne said "Mmmm" as she took another bite.

Alice said, "What boys?"

"What do you mean?" Anne looked up, still licking cherry sauce off her fork.

"What you said before," Alice said. "'Those boys were right.'"

"Oh. She meant those motorcycle boys," Anne said.

"Tiny and Boom," Mrs. B said. "They're the ones who told us how to get here. They really enjoyed your pie."

Alice said, "You know, I was so happy to have women company, I didn't even think to ask. What brought you all the way out here?"

Mrs. B had been thinking about this, and she was ready with an answer. "Someone tried to break into your house, through the cellar window. They didn't get in, but we thought you'd want to know. Your neighbor Patty stopped them."

"Did Patty know who it was?"

"She did," Mrs. B said. "A boy named Nicky. I don't remember his last name but it sounded Slovak."

Alice's face darkened. She put her head down and leaned on her elbow, hand to her forehead. "That's okay. I know who Nicky is." She sat for a minute, not saying anything. Then she got up and shut off the stove. She brought the open pot to the table and filled their cups, spilling a little bit as she poured. She wiped it up with a dishtowel, hung the towel on the oven door, and sat back in her chair.

"My girls," Alice said with a sigh. "My beautiful little girls. They were so sweet when their dad was alive. We were so proud of them, felt like we were doing everything right." She shook her head. "I thought they'd always be that way. Sweet." She took a sip of her tea, staring into space. Mrs. B and Anne quietly finished their pie.

Finally Alice broke the silence. "When Barry died, I didn't know what to do. Oh, I could fix things around the house, all that sort of thing, and we got enough money what with the social security and his life insurance. Barry's father died young, so when Theresa was born, first thing he did was go out and get life insurance. He wanted to make sure the girls were taken care of.

"So we were fine there. But I was so sad." Mrs. B and Anne both nodded sympathetically. "I couldn't mope around and cry all the time, like I wanted to, because I had to take care of the girls. I so wanted my little girls to be happy. I didn't want them to be sad. But our happy life just disappeared when Barry died.

"I went overboard, I guess. Barry was always the one who said 'no.' When Barry was alive, I never had to tell the girls 'no.' Then when he was gone, I tried to make a nice life for them, but it felt like they were mad at me all the time, no matter what I did." A tear rolled past her cheek and she wiped it with the side of her hand. "I tried so hard. I really tried, I really did."

Mrs. B reached out to hold Alice's hand. "No one looks back on their life and thinks they raised their children perfectly," she said. "No one does."

"You don't know," Alice said, shaking her head. "You don't know my girls. I didn't mean to, but I did wrong by them somehow."

"You did your level best." Mrs. B had given this a lot of thought over the years, and her words were gentle and certain. "I know what it's like. You go over and over it in your mind, how you might have done things differently, made things come out right. But none of us is that powerful, no matter how much we wish we were. Sometimes we hate that, and sometimes it hurts. Sometimes it hurts really bad." Mrs. B's eyes welled up as she went on, patting Alice's hand tenderly as she spoke. "You loved those girls, and you raised them the best you could. There comes a day that the road they take isn't up to you any more. It's up to them."

In the quiet that came afterward, Sparky wandered over to huddle on the floor between them. Alice looked down and scratched him under the chin. "My Maizie, she was my company for so many years. Cutest little thing. Mixed breed, not sure what. Golden colored, like this fellow. Think she had some cocker spaniel in her." Sparky's tail wagged faster and faster as she talked and, despite herself, Alice began to laugh. "And now Sparky here wants my attention. Don't you, Sparky? Don't you?"

Anne stood up and collected their dishes. As they rattled into the sink, she turned on the water and called over from the boot room, "Patty locked your cellar window."

"Oh, that's good," Alice said. "What Nicky's looking for isn't at the house anyhow, but he shouldn't be in there, going through my things. Anne, don't do those dishes. Come back and sit down." Alice went to the counter and gave a slice of cucumber to the dog. "Can you believe this dog likes cucumbers? Carrots I've seen, but never cucumbers. That's a new one on me."

She leaned on the sink, and the dog looked up for more. "No, no, Sparky, just one. You don't want to get a tummy ache." She bent down to scratch his neck, looking up at her friends. "I've got this good necklace, used to belong to my mother. My father gave it to Mom when they were dating. It's worth quite a bit of money. Mom had it appraised back when the girls were young, and the jeweler said it was worth $200,000. Can you believe it?

"But of course I would never sell it, because it came from my father. I keep it in a safety deposit box at that bank downtown, the one next to the William Penn Hotel. Every year when I go down to pay the rental bill, I look at the necklace for a while, hold it in my hand, think about my dad. I never knew him. I like to wonder what he was like. Then I treat myself to a cup of tea over in the lobby at the William Penn, at that nice restaurant there. I do that every year. Been doing it for a long time now. I wish I could take my girls, but you don't know how they are."

Anne said, "I haven't been to the William Penn in ages. The three of us should go sometime."

"Really?" Alice said. "Oh, that would be so nice! You know, I really had a good time at the Senior Center. There were ladies at the crafts table I hadn't seen since the girls were in school. And Carmella was there. She used to come over for coffee all the time before she moved away."

"We hope you'll come back to the Senior Center," Mrs. B said. "You know, I had the opportunity to meet your granddaughter the other day. She was playing with a little girl on my street. She seems like a lovely child."

Alice was all smiles. "Isn't she the sweetest thing? I don't get to see her much. When I had Maizie I would walk by her house, and sometimes she would come out for a few minutes if Theresa wasn't home. Her husband's a good man, Greg is, but I don't know how he puts up with my Theresa's temper."

I'll need to talk to Kelly tonight, Mrs. B thought, so she and Blossom can tell little Cassie that Alice is all right. What a shame Cassie can come to visit me but not her own grandmother, she thought. When Mrs. B was growing up, the little house she lived in was full of extended family, including her grandparents, like most of the homes on Polish Hill. It didn't seem fair that Cassie couldn't spend time with her grandma, not only for Alice's sake but for the child's sake, too. Mrs. B said, "Do you think Greg might bring Cassie downtown sometime, to meet you at the bank?"

Alice sat up straight for a moment, as if she were steeling herself. Then she softened. "Well, if Theresa never found out, it wouldn't hurt anyone, would it?" she said, her voice gathering excitement as she talked. "It would be so much fun to take Cassie to tea at the William Penn! We could get all dressed up. I'll bet she's never seen such a fancy place, and she'll love the waiters, how they pour your tea like you're somebody special, like you're royalty or something."

She went to the counter and then turned toward Sparky with another slice of cucumber. "You know, that wasn't Nicky's bright idea, breaking into my house. I know my Mary Jane. She put him up to it."

40

"I thought Alice might want to ride home with us," Mrs. B said as she settled into the passenger seat. "She did say she needs to get home to check on things at some point."

"I'm sure she wants to be back in her own clothes, too. I don't know what that woman sees in all that solar this and generator that," Anne said. "If I was on a date, the last thing I'd want to do is look at blueprints for a windmill."

"They do seem to be a match, don't they?" Mrs. B said.

Anne nodded. "He's sweet on her. You can't always tell by the way he talks, but you can see it when he looks at her."

It took almost an hour to get to their destination but it was a pleasant hour, traveling country roads and listening to the radio, the sun occasionally peeking out from puffy cumulus clouds.

"Look, there it is on the left." A big white sign announced *Sarris Chocolate Factory and Ice Cream Parlor.* They pulled into the parking lot and walked through double glass doors. The smell of chocolate and gumdrops washed over them like a tidal wave. They passed cases filled with homemade candies, a giant wall display of jellybeans. Mrs. B took hold of the red licorice-swizzle handrail and climbed three white tile stairs to the ice cream parlor. Anne was right behind her as they made their way to the counter to get in line.

"I can't believe we're buying ice cream. We just ate pie," Mrs. B said as she eyed the list of flavors on the wall behind the counter.

"Oh, one little dish won't hurt. We'll order a kid's scoop," Anne said. "What are you getting?"

Mrs. B looked at the menu one more time. "Whitehouse. What about you?"

"Rum Raisin," Anne said.

The place was busy. They carried the little round portions in their clear plastic bowls over to a table by the window, but by the time they reached it, it was already taken. They turned to look for another just as a young woman got up from a booth. She had a baby carrier on the table and a diaper bag over her shoulder. With her left hand she was attempting to pry a toddler's hand from a giant rhinestone on the back of the red padded booth. With her right hand, she was struggling to open a stroller.

Mrs. B set her ice cream on the table at the booth. She took the stroller from the woman and opened it, then held it still while the woman got her children situated. The baby in the carrier wiggled happily. "You have your hands full, don't you?" Mrs. B said.

"Wouldn't have it any other way," the woman laughed as she reached into her bag for a cloth to wipe chocolate from the toddler's face. Mrs. B and Anne waved to the baby while she did so.

"Mmm," Anne said when they'd settled into the booth and she took her first bite. Then she looked up to peer at Mrs. B. "Okay now. You have to tell me. How on earth did you know Alice met Harvey over by those berry bushes?"

Mrs. B picked up her white plastic spoon. "It just came to me in the middle of the night."

"What, like a psychic dream?" Anne made a face.

"Oh, don't be silly," Mrs. B said. "Did you watch *The Enchanted Cottage* last night?"

"Handsome Robert Young. I started to watch it but then my daughter called."

"The one who's mad at you for driving the convertible?"

Anne nodded. "She called from North Carolina. They're on vacation, down at my brother's condo. She called to let me know they got down there okay. First she's telling me about these funny t-shirts she saw on the boardwalk, and I think oh, good, she's having a good time, and then she starts complaining about her husband going golfing tomorrow and she's stuck cooking for everybody. Honestly, why go on vacation if you're going to complain? Just don't go. Stay home and let them cook for themselves. Or don't cook, and he'll get hungry and take you out. Or somebody else will cook. You don't have to be a genius to figure that out. I don't understand that girl at all. Anyhow, I can drive the convertible all this week while she's gone. I wrote Bobby a letter and told him I've been using it. I know my grandson. He'll get a kick out of picturing his old grandma driving his Mustang. What about your Helen? Is she still mad at you?"

"You know, Anne, I really don't know what to do. After all this with Alice, I know I'm lucky to have a daughter who cares about me the way my Helen does. I don't want her to be mad at me, I really don't. But I'm don't want to move away. I like my house, and I like Burchfield."

Anne took another bite of ice cream. "I don't want you to move away, either. What's all this about anyway, her wanting you to move?"

"Oh," Mrs. B shook her head, "she worries about everything. She thinks if I had someone watching over me every minute of the day, she wouldn't worry so much."

Anne took another bite. "Maybe you can get a cowbell and hang it around your neck so she knows where you are all the time."

"That's probably the only thing that would work." Mrs. B put her spoon down on the white rectangle of her paper napkin. "The sad thing is, if I did what Helen wants, if I moved to one of those old people's homes, she'd still worry. She'd find something else to worry about. Meanwhile, there I'd be, no more house, my independence gone, spending what precious time I have left with a bunch of strangers. So that's my choice. Move, or risk alienating my only daughter. Devil and the deep blue sea. I can't win this one for losing." She picked up the spoon again and took another bite.

Anne did the same. Then she waved her spoon in a little circle and said, "Weren't we talking about something before?"

"Your daughter?"

"No, before that."

"*The Enchanted Cottage*?" Mrs. B said.

"Yeah. Robert Young. Wait," Anne said. "When we got to the restaurant, you went right back to that path. Did you figure out that's where Alice was? Why didn't you tell me?"

"I didn't know for sure," Mrs. B said. She sat back in the booth for a moment. Her head tilted to the right, and she stared intently at the triple-scoop ice cream cone etched in the glass above her friend's head. "I woke up in the middle of the night, worrying," she said, "and I went over everything we knew about Alice, everything we did while we looked for her. So many things pointed in that direction, I don't know why I didn't see it before."

Mrs. B ticked items off on her fingers as she spoke. "Alice's workshop in her cellar. That was a clue. The Mother Earth News magazines in her living room, the ones about running self-sufficient farms just like Harvey's. That was another clue. That path down the hill was right behind the restaurant. And where was the last place anyone saw Alice last Sunday? *At the restaurant.*" As she said each of the last three words, she tapped the table with her forefinger for emphasis. "Alice left the table to go to the ladies room, and we never found a *single* person who saw her after that. And remember, when we went to look for her, the back door was open, and those berry bushes were right outside. And what was the first thing we did when we saw them?" She looked Anne in the eye, still pointing her finger as she spoke. "We went right over there. So doesn't it make sense that Alice would have? And the path was right there. The woman at the store last week said Harvey ate tiger lilies. So it sounded like he would forage. We were eating those berries, and it made sense he would too."

Mrs. B picked up her spoon again. "Of course, I couldn't be sure. On the one hand, it seemed like such a stretch. But the more I thought about it, the more possible it seemed. Watching *The Enchanted Cottage* on television that night didn't hurt anything. That might have made me think of it. So I wasn't sure, by any means. But it all seemed to make sense."

"I can't believe you put that all together. I don't know how you remember all those little details of what people say," Anne said.

Mrs. B said, "I really should have known early on that it was a possibility. Instead I got all worried about Alice, and I dragged you in, too. I guess I can be as bad as Helen sometimes."

"You didn't drag me into anything," Anne said. "If you wouldn't have gone looking for Alice with me, I would have done it alone, I was so worried. And it was much more fun this way. Now I feel like Nancy Drew after she solved the mystery." She scraped the last of the rum raisin ice cream from the bottom of her plastic bowl, then set down her spoon and pointed a pale pink fingernail toward the entrance. "We have to go see Perry Como. He's right around here somewhere. But before that, I need to stop over at the candy counter. There's a Sen-Sen display next to the cash register."

The ladies sat in contented silence for a minute or two while Mrs. B enjoyed the last few bites of her cherry vanilla ice cream. Finally Anne said, "Meeting Harvey seems to have done Alice a world of good. But she's got to go home soon and get some decent clothes. She's dressing like a ragamuffin."

41

Anne pulled up in front of an antique store so they could park in the shade, half a block from the white town square where Perry Como's statue held court eternally, surrounded by marble benches and occasional adoring fans. In the window of the antique store was a large porcelain doll. "Oh, I had one of those!" Anne said.

Next to it was another doll. That one was smaller, and its hair was matted. "Some little girl loved this one," Mrs. B said.

Anne pointed at a brass cowbell. "Here you go, Ed. All you need now is a ribbon to hang it around your neck."

Mrs. B studied the cowbell, imagined the feel of the battered metal. Something was important about that cowbell. What was it? She imagined the *clong, clong* sound it would make and the thought triggered something in the back of her mind. While they walked toward the Perry Como statue, she mulled it over. It was something… something about a necklace. Not Alice's necklace. No, another one. Not a pretty necklace. Maybe not a necklace. What was it? Something… from television? Was it something she saw on television?

The sun went behind a large cloud. By the time they reached the town square the temperature had dropped a little and, sitting in front of the statue on a marble bench, the women were comfortably cool.

"Nice they dressed him in a sweater and chinos," Anne said.

"It wouldn't have been right to have him dressed to the nines," Mrs. B said. "He was always so down-to-earth."

The ladies sat for a while, watching the handsome white statue sing his silent song. The brick pavement underneath their feet was wet. Someone must have hosed it down earlier.

"Always looked forward to Perry Como on Channel 11," Anne said finally.

What on earth was it she saw on the television? Mrs. B asked herself. Something about Helen, she thought. Something about a necklace...

Then it came to her, and Mrs. B sighed as if she'd just set down a heavy shopping bag. Yes, she thought. It will work. She knew it would work. She knew how to make things right with her daughter.

She reached over and gave Anne's hand a series of quick taps. "You know what?"

"Tell me," Anne said, reaching into her purse for the Sen-Sen. She tore open the packet and offered it to Mrs. B, then poured a few black specks into the palm of her outstretched hand.

Mrs. B said, "I'm writing a letter to my Helen tonight when we get home. I'm going to ask her to get me one of those things you wear around your neck, the ones that call 9-1-1 when you press the button."

Anne looked at her sideways. "You don't need that," she said as she popped the candy into her mouth. "That's for old people."

"We're old people."

"Oh, you know what I mean."

Mrs. B said, "You're right, I need it like a hole in the head. But won't it make Helen happy? She'll feel like someone's watching over me. She'll have her cowbell."

The sun came out, and she smiled. It was going to be all right.

Eventually, the ladies got up and walked back to the car. Mrs. B felt different now. An odd sensation, and it was a while before she could name it. But as she sat in the passenger seat of the baby blue Mustang, tying the flowered babushka around her white hair, it came to her.

Free, is what it felt like.

This week being the rare exception, Mrs. B was seldom in a car nowadays. Jimmy took her to the grocery store once a month, maybe two times if a holiday was coming. He was kind to do that. Jimmy was a good neighbor. But he had a practical car. Mrs. B didn't know what kind it was. Nondescript. A four-door sedan. Beige.

But this car was a treat. Anne's grandson's convertible, the seats already hot when she got in, even though Anne was so careful to park in the shade. The feel of this soft ivory leather upholstery—was it leather? It felt like leather. Vinyl always had that sticky, shiny feel. This was like sinking into a chair made of tapioca pudding. It had to be leather. And the beautiful dashboard with its big round gauges. Anne did keep the car so nice, all shiny chrome, and the color was a lovely baby blue, like the buttons on the Easter hat Mrs. B wore in seventh grade.

It felt a teeny bit wrong, an old lady like her, sitting in this car obviously made for young people. A boy and girl should be sitting here, all fresh-faced and bold, the girl in a wide pleated skirt and the blouse she tried on three times before she decided it was the right one, the boy sneaking a look in the rear view mirror to see if his hair still looked the way it should, so proud of his car, wondering if the girl would have gone out with him if he didn't have the car, hoping she would.

That's who's supposed to be in this car, thought Mrs. B. Not me. Not an old lady, sitting in the passenger side with her good, good friend in the driver's side, two old ladies tooling around in a car made for young folks.

It *was* beautiful, though. It did feel good, the top down, the wind in her hair. She pulled the babushka farther down on her white bangs, tied it a little bit tighter under her chin. The scarf flapped when they entered the parkway and began to pick up speed. And there they were, flying along like two beautiful birds in a beautiful blue car. They were young again, for a moment, she and Anne. Two young women, carefree and full of energy.

Anne reached over and turned on the radio, and Perry Como's smooth tenor came through the speakers. Mrs. B and Anne laughed as they began to sing along.

www.brandtstreetpress.com

Would you like us to let
you know when a new
Mrs. B Mystery is available?

Email us at
MrsB@brandtstreetpress.com